Mexico Road

Mexico Road

A Novel

Gary Ludwig

Basket Road Press
Harrisburg, PA 17111

Second Edition
2008

To order additional books contact:
info@basketroadpress.com

To Beth,

and Christine.

In memory of

Marcia and John,

Mom and Dad.

The message from M.D.H.

"Allegory"

Max Liebermann, *"Dadchen aus Laren"*
© Artists Rights Society (ARS),
New York/VG Bild-Kunst, Bonn

Chapter 1

The Pennsylvania German influence on the cultural history of rural communities in Southeastern Pennsylvania has been deep-rooted for 275 years. Here, for generations, farming has provided the simplicity of life many yearn for. Many times illusory stone walls, thicker and higher than usually imagined, and made impenetrable by an almost secret silent code of ancestral behavior, are built to cuddle the ambitions of the young and the contentment of the aged, and to shelter those savoring success and others coping with failure. Their obsession with privacy causes them to turn their heads the other way so their neighbors also will, and many tremble when thinking of the shame that'd surely come if the assortment of sins, theirs and others, some small, some bigger, and even those horrid, are exposed.

The Oregon Inn, a picturesque idyllic country hotel owned by the Hartman family for generations, is situated about ten miles from Rossville, Pennsylvania, a city of about 60,000 people.

Nestled among the thick trees of the pine forest in a rural, closed-off haven that touches the base of the beautiful and tranquil Blue Mountains, the inn lies at the south end of the unpaved road called Mexico Road. About one mile away, halfway to the north end, is the village of Alton Manor, a cluster of small cottages—homes to about one hundred families, most of them of German ancestry, bilingual—speaking heavily accented English and the Pennsylvania Dutch dialect. The village has three churches, a country store and gas station, a tavern, and a thriving farmer's market. In between the two ends of the road lie a half dozen or so small farms fronting it, most producing fruits and vegetables, but some have small herds of cattle or broiler houses full of chickens.

The local people have long suspected soldiers returning in 1848 from the Mexican War named the dirt road as a tribute to their war service. It takes nearly constant effort to fill in the ruts and puddles on the white limestone surface that turns into a sticky paste when wet. When drivers bounce their cars over the water-filled potholes, they splash the chalky, watery mess so high it reaches their windshields and any pedestrians who fail to run off into the wood's edge to get out of reach. During the summer, when the road becomes dried out, speeding cars launch large white clouds of dust into the air. Someone standing in the midst of this haze could easily be reminded of his or her school days cleaning the blackboard erasers, choking and coughing from the fallout settling in their throats.

The Hartman family immigrated to America in 1737 from Germany. In 1893, after of the family farmed for generations the virgin fertile land, patriarch Reuben Hartman built the Oregon Inn of wood cut from the mature pine and oak trees that towered over his land. Teams of horses dragged the logs four miles away to the sawmill where they were rough-cut into boards. As soon as the huge stone foundation was laid, the lumber was brought back from the sawmill on wagons and fashioned into a large two-story inn that'd look quite archetypal in the German Alps.

Reuben and his wife Sarah named the hotel the Oregon Inn after a small log tavern that once stood on the same spot before being abandoned after the Civil War. Legend has it that a dozen or so of the local men, instead of coming home after the Mexican War ended in 1848, went to the newly created Oregon Territory after hearing that free government land would be offered. Fighting the Native Americans, who had claims to the territory, made them reluctant to send for their wives. They all gave up and came home before the Oregon Donation Land Act of 1850 was enacted, naming the tavern to mark their misadventures.

Reuben, a cattle dealer and farmer with increasing wealth, had earlier decided a good investment would be a small hotel and barroom—a country retreat where affluent families from Rossville and other nearby cities could get relief from the summer heat and humidity, enjoy the tree shaded days and cool tranquil nights, and indulge in good food, lodging, and service.

He used his workers and hired a few extras to do the building. The roof was extended to cover a large porch that surrounds the entire second floor, and then furnished with large wooden rocking chairs with cushioned seats for the guests to sit in and savor their freedom from toil and strain, partaking the sights and sounds of this small, serene paradise.

Fifteen rooms were decorated exactly alike, featuring gray wall covering with a floral imprint of red roses and green leaving, matching fringed rugs covering the rough planed wooden floor, and attractively furnished with thick beds with oak headboards draped with white mosquito netting. The cozy rooms each had a chest of drawers, writing desk and chair, and an overstuffed easy chair with reading lamp. An able staff catered to the guests with utmost efficiency. Large screened, wood-framed windows allowed the summer night breezes inside, carrying with them the pure and natural smells of the dense, deep-rooted woods. Steeples with weather vanes sat atop a huge white barn with a livery stable and carriage house out back, manned by experienced attendants—necessary given that guests would come in beautiful black lacquered carriages, drawn by sleek horses dressed in fancy leather tack and plumes and steered by neatly uniformed teamsters.

The inn still features a small lobby at the first-floor entrance, furnished with a waiting room settee, a small registration desk, and a large rug similar to the ones originally laid in the rooms upstairs. The door to the right leads to the barroom, the one to the left to the dining room, and straight ahead is the large wooden staircase leading upstairs. The barroom features a large fifteen-feet-long walnut bar with ornate carvings with a top sanded and varnished to a smooth shiny finish. The plaster walls, painted tan, and the white sculptured ceiling made of stamped tin squares complement the large walnut cabinets in back of the bar, all this installed when the inn was built—unaffordable if purchased in these modern days. The cabinets, also featuring woodcarvings, start at the floor and reach to the high ceiling. They contain compartment doors and drawers with mounted decorative clear glass, brass handles, polished brass lamps, beveled, fancy etched mirrors, and shelves to hold the liquor. In the earlier days the men just stood at the bar, resting their boots on the brass foot rail, and matching spittoons were spaced along the floor. Later, as customs changed, barstools were added. The dining room originally featured crushed red velvet wall covering, about twenty round oak tables, and chairs with round oak seats and black wrought-iron backs and legs. Four large chandeliers lit the room, each containing twelve gild-edged milk-glass lamps. At dinner a candle was lit at each table for intimacy. In the far corner was a small eight-foot-by-eight-foot stage with a small dance floor in front of it. Eventually the room was given updated furnishings to conform to changing styles—oak tables and chairs gave way to plastic and chrome.

Reuben and Sarah's youngest child, Adam, and his wife Mary were the next generation to run the inn, and under their management it prospered and soon achieved a fine reputation.

Adam and Mary's oldest son, Allen, was born in 1898 and married Katie in 1918. They became the third generation of innkeepers in 1919 just before Prohibition. After its repeal in

1933 they recognized that because automobiles were becoming more dependable and affordable, people no longer were interested in coming to their inn to escape the city—they wanted to travel to the New Jersey shore, or to the Pocono and Catskill Mountains. Al, a shy and quiet man, was ill at ease dealing with strangers. He did his cattle dealing and left the running of the inn to Katie, who adeptly led the transformation of the inn from upscale resort to a barroom and restaurant serving the local community.

She began renting most of the rooms by the week or month to local bachelors, relying on traveling salesmen, tourists, or people visiting relatives in the area for only a small part of the income from lodging. She rented the barn to a local farmer who needed additional space to store hay and equipment. As a consequence, the rental income and Katie's good food kept the inn profitable and even got it through Prohibition.

Katie was a thin feisty woman back then, with short dark brown hair, her brown eyes got help from plastic pink-framed eyeglasses. She could hold her own when dealing with purveyors, haggling over prices and demanding good service. She acted swiftly when confronted by rowdy barroom patrons, mostly by shouting louder than any of them. Instances were rare, but if she were forced, she'd swing the baseball bat she kept behind the bar within an inch of the head of any out-of-control drunk. She had placed a sign on the mirror behind the bar that warned no profanity was allowed, and anybody thrown out of the place was never allowed back. No exceptions, ever. The inn's reputation for family dining and comfortable lodging was preserved because Katie ran the place with an iron fist— seldom standing still for more than a minute or two.

In 1919, the same year her and Al took over the inn, Katie gave birth to William, who was called Will. Katie had insisted that he go to college—she felt that her only child shouldn't stake his future on running a hotel and barroom that was fast becoming a rooming house. Will chose to become a military man, graduating from West Point in 1941. He served in World War II gallantly in the bloody battles of the Philippines and Okinawa. In June 1943 he came home for a thirty-day furlough before being sent to Europe.

Jonas Konrad, one of Will's high school classmates, was a short man with a narrow pointed nose too large for his tiny face and a prematurely receded hairline of thin blond hair. The Konrad farm adjoined the Hartman's. Jonas had become, like his father Fritz, a Nazi sympathizer and then a supporter. When he showed up at the inn drunk during Will's homecoming party he stumbled through the doorway, shouting, "Send out the war hero, I wanna see how tough he is fighting with his fists. Let's see how much guts he has when he doesn't have his gun." Two men, who were in the barroom drinking, came over to the dining room after hearing his shouting and took him home and put him to bed.

The Konrads were bitter enemies of the Hartman family since 1915 when Hartman cattlemen refused to sell Fritz some quality breeding livestock on credit. He blamed them for bringing about his failure in the cattle business.

Jonas had always been jealous of Will's fine looks, his success in sports, and the good grades and popularity he had all through school, and of course his appointment to West Point. He resented the community honoring the young officer for his service in the Pacific at community functions and became outraged when he read in the newspaper that Will was going to Europe to fight the cause that he and his father fervently supported and believed in, Adolph Hitler's design for the world. After reading the news accounts he drank for two days. The whiskey is what gave him the courage to go to the inn to taunt his former school chum.

The community had admonished the Konrads for their beliefs, but because of the patriotic fervor that the nation was caught up in, they never suspected that anyone they knew, even Jonas, would refuse to fight for their country. He would've refused and willingly gone to jail if he had been drafted, but he was given a hardship deferment because Fritz suffered debilitating back injuries. Jonas was needed to run the family farm.

In June 1943, while home on the furlough, Will married Magdalena Ligorio, his girlfriend since their sophomore year in high school. He had become a handsome man, six foot two inches tall. He wore his sandy brown hair short on the sides like all army officers, but long on the top, parted on the side and combed across. He had a boyish face—clean-shaven with a ruddy complexion and penetrating gray eyes. Magdalena was five feet tall and wore her black hair short, held close around her beautifully proportioned face with its olive skinned complexion, highlighted by her large and beautiful round dark brown eyes. Their as yet to be born son, whom they had decided to name Seth, was conceived before Will departed for Europe. Three days before he was scheduled to leave, he received notification that he had been promoted to lieutenant colonel. Ever since that day, Will has been known as Colonel Hartman, even after leaving the army. Magdalena moved into the Oregon Inn and spent her time being pregnant and getting to know Katie, her new mother-in-law. She helped clean rooms, lent a hand in the kitchen, and prayed for her husband's safety while waiting nervously for his return.

Magdalena was from an Italian immigrant family. Her father and mother came to America after World War I and went into the mushroom business. Antonio and Maria Ligorio didn't want their daughter to marry Will, but she disobeyed them and married him anyway. The Ligorios had continued to practice their old-world lifestyle, following the Italian customs, and they felt their daughter was betraying her culture and faith by marrying a Pennsylvania German who wasn't Catholic.

Practically all the Italian immigrants of the early 20th century, including those that settled in this area of Pennsylvania, were discriminated against because they were poor and didn't speak English—and they reacted by creating and maintaining their closed society. To make matters worse, the ones that were growing mushrooms had most of the residents of the Rossville area turned against them because of the foul odor that filled the night air near their mushroom barns. The stink emanated from the sun-heated manure that was spread out over the beds of buried mushrooms that can grow only in warm darkness.

They were cordial to Will, respecting his family's wealth and appreciating that he was able to provide financial security for their daughter, but they never would accept him as a member of their family.

On March 13, 1944, Magdalena died from complications while giving birth to Seth at the Rossville General Hospital. She was nineteen years old. Will was devastated. He never imagined he'd be forced to live through the tragedy of losing his young and healthy wife.

Magdalena's sister, Henrietta Messaro, came to the Oregon Inn to help Katie run things and take care of the newborn infant. Henrietta had always supported her sister marrying Will, faulting her parents for their refusal to accept him as their son-in-law, and now, Seth as their grandson. However, being raised in a strict Italian family taught her to keep focused on the work that needed to be done, choosing not to discuss anything that could rouse or further aggravate family disputes. She resembled her sister, thin, five feet tall with short black hair and olive complexion, beautiful brown eyes highlighting her pretty face. She was the older sister, not shy like Magdalena, and because she was built well enough, she entered beauty pageants during her school days. She attracted men, even younger men, but she married an older one. Sal Messaro, a soft-spoken man, was seven years older, short—5' 10", with black hair and receding hairline—always wore long-sleeve white dress shirts, black pants, and black pointed Italian shoes. His parents, like the Ligorios, had emigrated from Italy after the turn of the century, carrying along with them the thick ethnic traditions and language of the old country, a sustained way of life that he was born into and now lived as an adult. He owned two restaurants in Rossville—came to the inn only on weekends, but mostly he was a racketeer, a local mobster. Henrietta met him while working as a waitress at one of his restaurants when she was still in high school. After they were married, the doctor told them that she'd never have children. She was distraught and he shrugged his shoulders. Later he told her, "It's not my problem—deal with it." They never spoke again about her being barren.

For the next six years Katie and Henrietta worked together raising Seth, sharing the responsibility without any discord. They both loved the child—as he grew older it became obvious he was Italian and German—growing to be a handsome boy with black curly hair, brown eyes, and dark olive skin like his mother's, made darker by the summer sun, and his father's straight rigid German nose, prominent forehead and sturdy chin—classic looks indeed. Katie knew that the boy filled a void in Henrietta's life, and she was happy for her, while Henrietta understood that Katie was protecting the interests of the Hartman family and would do whatever was necessary to insure that he inherited the Oregon Inn. The cultural differences of the two women in many ways enhanced Seth's development. Katie instilled in him the traditions of the Pennsylvania Germans—work hard, be practical and thrifty. Henrietta tutored him in the Mediterranean lifestyle, the food, the appreciation of music and art, and the beauty of ceremony in the Catholic Church. Many people, until they were corrected, thought that he was her son. Both women knew how much special handling it was going to take to raise him in the environment that was beginning to exist at the inn.

He started school on a cold and windy September morning in 1950, walking the half-mile or so to Antietam Road, the main road that crossed Mexico Road, where the old yellow rickety school bus picked him up. School and television, both new to him, awoke a great deal of curiosity, sharpening his senses, he was becoming much more perceptive while living his boyhood and recording the memories—experiencing the smell of hay in the barns and the wheat in the fields. He recalled standing in front of the wood- and coal-burning stoves that stood in each of the main rooms before the inn got a central heating system, the radiant heat hitting his face while he stood close to it warming his hands. He remembered watching the escaping smoke, with its unmistakable smell of burning wood, spewing from the chimneys atop the inn and the cottages in Alton Manor. After the inn's coal burning boiler was installed in 1951, he'd wait for the sulfur smell to permeate from the heat vents throughout the whole building every night while Katie or Henrietta were down in the basement "slacking the furnace", shaking the grates to rid them of the ashes

During summer nights, when the Mexico Road neighborhood was blessed with a warm breeze, bestowing relief from the day's heat and humidity, Seth often sat on a rocking chair on the second story porch—beginning when he was so young his feet barely touched the floor. He'd listen, while rocking back and forth, to the crickets chirping, and watch the cornstalks sway in the field with their long leaves and tassels fluttering as the air rushed by.

In those days electric service was interrupted more frequently when severe summer thunderstorms or winter snowstorms came. The Hartmans, like many other families, had kerosene "coal oil" lamps, left over from the days before there was electric service, now used during those urgent weather conditions. The inn owned many more than the average family because only thirty years earlier the entire inn was lit by them. They were kept alongside the table linens and silverware in a large closet in the dining room, the pungent smell of pent-up mothballs assaulting the room whenever its big wooden doors were opened. During the winter storm's hours of cold and darkness, with the flickering flames from the lamps reflecting off the walls and ceiling, and the howling wind blowing the snow into huge drifts, Seth snuggled under heavy heirloom quilts and blankets, feeling transported back into an earlier era. Suddenly the stories he heard the local patrons tell about the old days began to have a closer feeling. They told of the Sunday school picnics where literally hundreds of people attended. They told stories about his great-great-grandparents Reuben and Sarah Hartman, and his great-grandparents and grandparents who carried on the traditions of the Hartman family. The talk sent Seth's mind back to an era that was far more recent than a young boy's comprehension of time realizes.

When Reuben Hartman's life was studied in Seth's fourth grade local history class, his classmates giggled because the man being discussed had the same last name as his. A quiet ambiance overcame the class when schoolteacher Carl Dengler, a distinguished-looking man with thick gray hair and very bushy eyebrows, an old Hartman family friend, revealed to the group that Seth was a descendant of the man who paid for the school building, originally a one-room schoolhouse. Updated, remodeled, and added on to many times since then, it now had six classrooms—each teacher taught two grades. Dengler taught them that Reuben was born in 1837, his brother William in 1840. Both were drafted and fought in the Civil War. William, wounded in July 1863 at Gettysburg, was brought home and died the following month in the same bed he had slept in from the time he left the crib. Because Reuben had taught himself to play the piano and the flute, he was assigned duty as a musician in a regiment that did mostly sentry and ceremonial duty and saw very little combat.

Reuben and Sarah were married in 1856—they led active lives while raising their children, four daughters and three sons. Family members learned how intensely loyal they were to each other when her diary was discovered in an old trunk when the farm and long stored family memorabilia was divided among family members. Dengler was asked to translate the diary from German to English.

Readers learned that the patriarch of his family served on the board of directors of local banks and church, community, and government boards and commissions—he was truly a leader who could speak, read, and write English, but like most people in the community during that era, he talked German in the "Pennsylvania Dutch" dialect. Seth's learning about his family in school planted the seed that developed into his passionate family pride. In 1956 that emergent family pride was casehardened when Dengler, on the day of his retirement, gave Seth a translated copy of the diary. He sat at a table in the dining room and began to read it; each day he learned more about his ancestors.

In the book, Sarah describes how Reuben became wealthy. "He worked hard and had a flair for business." In her introduction she says, "He's loud, boisterous, and aggressive, but also has integrity, is fair, forthright, and honest, in many ways typical of a Pennsylvania German-American farmer." She gives a warm, loving, and pointed description of the man of her life. "He's big and husky with steel gray eyes, a ruddy complexion with deep wrinkles in his forehead reminding us of his maturity, he's always clean-shaven, and has thick coarse chestnut hair that he parts and combs back, but always looking windswept. He wears bib overalls, wool plaid shirts, and big brown high boots. For church and meetings he wears a gray suit, white shirt, and necktie."

Sarah was from a prominent milling family in the nearby town of Leshville. A portrait of her that still hangs in the inn's lobby shows she was small and dainty and had fine facial features, blue eyes and blonde hair that she pinned back. She wrote, "I wear long plain dresses, but for church and social events I wear beautiful silk dresses with many petticoats, and stylish hats that transform me into a fashionable woman."

In the vivid and romantic memoir she discloses, "We're very dedicated to each other. Our marriage is based on loyalty, honesty, and we're truly very much in love." Surprisingly,

Sarah's written account of her adult life is much more revealing than would be expected from a nineteenth-century women, less inhibited because she was writing to herself and probably never suspected that anyone in future years would be interested in reading about her. She probably planned, and then forgot when she grew old, to destroy the book that included the most personal intimacies of her marriage. "He asks me if I feel well, and with my affirmation, he tells me that we shall go to bed and make love. I wrap my legs around him as he goes inside me, and we're one for hours." She confidently states, "I understand him like nobody else, I feel that I'm the prominent source of the self-confidence he possesses."

She describes their daily life—"Reuben works every day from 5 AM until 10 PM. On weekends he plays music, we dance, eat heartily, play with our children and go to church to thank God for the blessings of our lives. He leads the choir from his seat as the organist."

The gigantic Hartman farm was divided up in 1920 among all Reuben Hartman's descendants. The extended Hartman family was growing—there were cousins who now had families and wanted land to build their houses.

Chapter 2

Fritz Konrad, the Hartman's stern neighbor, had become a Nazi sympathizer by 1936.

He was a demanding and unyielding man with dirty blond hair—a deep resonant voice—he resembled the Bolshevik leader Vladimir Lenin. He had that remarkable face with a fierce expression, giving suspicious looks with his penetrating gray eyes. He wore the Cossack-style cap that Lenin wore—it allowed him to emulate the harsh Cossack lifestyle, eating a sparse diet, using horses to farm instead of modern equipment, having one large wood-burning stove in the kitchen for cooking and heating the whole farmhouse, and a small amount of well-worn second hand furniture.

He'd have adjusted quite well if thrown back in time to live with the Cossack serfs, who fled from the principality of Muscovy in the fourteenth and fifteenth centuries and established wheat-growing and stock-raising communities in Siberia, where everyone shared equally in the wealth. He believed a similar way of life that was forced upon his German ancestors by necessity in the eighteenth and nineteenth centuries was a route to peace and longevity, and living a similar lifestyle was his way of protesting to those he felt were corrupting the world.

The Konrad house, a large two-story stone structure built in the mid-nineteenth century, was always damp and cold. The floors were covered in every room, except the kitchen, with large old rugs of different colors and shapes Fritz had brought home from estate auctions. The kitchen had worn out linoleum flooring and was furnished with a large round oak table with un-matching chairs, picked up here and there, and a small old secondhand refrigerator. The house had no indoor plumbing— a hand pump that drew water from the outside well was mounted on the large chipped white porcelain sink, enabling Selma, his wife, to pump water into pots and washbasins. A large built-in wood chest stored the damp, moldy wood that was burned in the stove. Stacks of old newspapers and bundles of fresh Nazi literature waiting to be distributed were everywhere. Bathroom facilities consisted of an outhouse in the backyard. It took over a dozen cats to control the mouse and rat population.

Fritz demanded Selma keep house and raise Jonas in this unhealthy environment. She was a timid and shy woman in her middle forties, short and fragile, weighing about 100 pounds. She had blue eyes and long straight blond hair reaching to the bottom of her back that she wore hanging or at times braided. She always looked tired and worn, a victim of fatigue not only from hard work, but also from physical and emotional abuse Fritz inflicted on her.

His insistence on primitive farming, coupled with the time he spent on Nazi party activities, meant little money was earned to buy food, clothing, and other necessities. He had a college education—trained to be a schoolteacher, but because he was very outspoken about his white supremacist beliefs, no school board would hire him. So he farmed, manhandling his workhorses, disrupting local government meetings, writing scathing letters to the editor of the newspaper, and he ran for political office—always unsuccessfully—promoting radical ideas. He was always proclaiming that demands for change were part of a conspiracy by the Jews and other minorities to take over America and later the world. He wrote and spoke that social changes currently taking place must be halted, or the white race will be wiped out, bringing about the end of civilization.

As American involvement in the war became more and more certain, and the Nazi threat increased, more and more of Konrad's neighbors were beginning to shun him. People in the Alton Manor community were starting to believe he should be imprisoned.

He had wanted to buy Hartman land for many years that bordered a stream flowing into ten-acre Lorraine Lake, giving the Hartmans' cattle abundant water to drink. The Konrad farm didn't border any streams—water for Konrad livestock had to be pumped from wells, an expensive and time consuming process that never provided an adequate supply.

When the Hartmans were dividing their farm into smaller parcels in 1920, Fritz made an offer to buy a small strip of pastureland leading from his farm to the stream, but members of the extended Hartman family, brothers, sisters, aunts, uncles, and cousins, all part owners turned him down. This rejection, and their refusal to loan him money years earlier, denied Fritz a chance to build a profitable cattle business and increase the value of his farm. Their rejections planted the seeds of hatred he had for all Hartmans.

The Hartman farmhouse, barn, outbuildings and about seventy-five acres, including all the land bordering the stream, was given to Will's Aunt Mary and her husband, because they had run the family cattle business up until the end. The remaining one hundred and fifty acres were set aside to give five-acre parcels to family members to build houses.

Two days after Mary and her husband became the sole owners of the farm, the large barn burned to the ground. Seventeen milk cows and four horses were lost, along with hay, straw, and expensive equipment. Everyone knew that Fritz was the perpetrator but the police had no proof.

When prohibition ended in 1933 he attempted to strike more vengeance, hiring a lawyer to file a lawsuit to prevent the reopening of the inn's barroom, claiming it would create a nuisance to the Mexico Road community. The lawsuit was thrown out, but Konrad had accomplished what he set out to do—cost the Hartmans time and money.

Fritz became a dramatic and major influence over his son, preaching racial hatred to him at an early age. He was a harsh father, a strict disciplinarian, always critical of his attempts to do well in school or doing his farm work, rarely giving the boy any praise.

All the boys at school had farm work to do, but Jonas was burdened with five to six hours every day. While Will was physically conditioning himself playing sports, Jonas developed his muscular build doing agonizing, backbreaking labor, then collapsing into his bed about 10 PM, too tired to do his homework. In the morning at the breakfast table Selma would help her son do it, nervously watching out the window for the tyrant to come in from the barn for breakfast, knowing he'd go into a tirade if he found out the boy wasn't keeping up. Jonas made sure his mother knew he tried his best. "I got too tired and fell asleep with my clothing on." Every morning, with little deviation, Fritz would look at the clock, then snarl, "I'm gonna kick your goddamn ass if you don't get it moving!" Without ado, Jonas jumped from his chair and grabbed his books, leaping for the door, running across the porch and out the lane in what seemed like one swift move, as if made airborne by a large gust of wind.

He figured out that perhaps the only hope he had to become a good son and win his father's approval was to show an interest in Nazi party activities, and he soon developed a sincere belief in the demented doctrine. Fritz would've realized early if his son lacked sincerity. Despite their tumultuous relationship, Fritz and Jonas eventually bonded because they shared the view that whites are the only intelligent people on Earth, and that Jews and blacks and other minorities are the scourge of humanity.

Jonas and Will Hartman started school in 1925. They grew up a mile apart but weren't allowed to play together outside of school because of the feud between their families. They fought many times after Fritz convinced Jonas that Will's success came at the expense of Konrads. When Will graduated from West Point, destined to go off to war, Jonas's jealousy intensified.

He remembered while growing up his father beating his mother, yelling to him, "Get your ass out of here, and don't come back until I call for you." He dutifully went outside and took a walk far enough away from the house so the thick nighttime air and the loud chirping crickets would muffle his mother's cries and moans. Hearing his mother's suffering sounds as his father punched her haunted him all his life. He remembered when he was twelve years old she suffered a broken arm from yet another beating and he walked with her out Mexico Road on a frigid cold and windy winter day to the doctor. During the years he would notice his mother's bruises, broken teeth, black eyes, and cracked ribs, but eventually became convinced that if she had tried harder to please and respect her husband, she would've been spared the violence.

Fritz always raped her, sexually aroused only when he could dominate her and inflict physical and emotional pain, never caring for her or showing any affection, even when they were first married. He was a cold cruel man, but she kept hoping that someday he'd realize if he started to care for her, and learned to act on it, she'd love him back and he'd become a decent man. When she met him nobody warned her he treated women that way. He'd force her to sleep on the kitchen table the entire night as punishment for displeasing him. Perhaps she didn't cook his meal the way he liked, or didn't launder a certain pair of workpants. He'd get out of bed a few times during the night to make sure she was still atop it—he'd hear her sobs, telling to stop or he'd beat her in the morning.

Beneath Selma's haggard appearance was some natural beauty—she never wore any makeup, forbidden by Fritz. When seen at the market, she was usually smiling, talking to everyone, speaking very softly and always inquiring about the well being of other's family and friends. People didn't suspect she was living in a hell on earth.

She didn't agree with her husband and son's politics, but she would never be allowed to express her dissent without enduring yet more abuse.

One chilly spring morning in 1937, slowly drinking a cup of coffee while sitting on the porch rocking chair, she drifted into a deep state of emotional despair. The birds singing, busy gathering to build their nests, and the sweet smell of blooming flowers and rising grass, were of no help. She had been having trouble sleeping and eating, often shaking and throwing up, and had frequent thoughts of dying. Only a stubborn will saved her, she was able to talk herself out of her morbid feelings to conclude that she didn't have to live such a life. For her it was heart wrenching to watch Fritz brainwash their eighteen-year-old son, the child she loved so much. She named him Jonas because it was a name from the Bible. She was proud to present her husband with a son, and now he was turning him into a monster.

Finally concluding that she couldn't live with him any longer—if she stayed she'd be jeopardizing her very life—she somehow got the courage to leave with a handsome man who lived in Alton Manor. Fritz had never allowed her to get an office job, or to train as a hospital worker—even to work as a cook or waitress, so she came to believe she couldn't survive without him. The man that was giving her a once-in-a-lifetime chance for a new start was fifty-one years old and worked as a bookkeeper for the local sawmill. His wife had been ill for over a year and Selma had been hired to care for her. When she died he asked her to stay on and help with the household chores for a few months, coming early in the morning for a few hours, and then returning in the evening to prepare and serve him his evening meal.

That January it snowed off and on for days, then came the freezing rain. Frigid temperatures caused everyone to bundle up in their heaviest wraps. He came home from work early to shovel snow and knock down the large, dangerous icicles hanging from the roof's storm gutters, then came inside to sip steaming hot chocolate that Selma had prepared. They talked small talk about the weather and then he told her he was offered a very good job in Philadelphia and he wanted her to go with him. Selma gasped—she was shocked speechless. She never had any romantic thoughts about him.

She suspected he was having a reaction from grief—surely a widower wouldn't be interested in another woman already! And why would he want her? He had always been kind to her, treating her with respect, never doing or saying anything improper, but did he want sex so badly that he'd try to seduce a worn out farmer's wife? Or did he just want her to accompany him as his housekeeper? She ruled that out after realizing he could hire a woman in Philadelphia to keep house.

During the following months he never pressured her, only occasionally reminding her during other conversations that he'd like her to leave with him. She was surprised that he could ask a married woman to commit to him without feeling guilty, but he knew she was being abused and living a tragic existence. Before long she was developing feelings for him, but began to worry about him hurting her. She finally came to accept that he was making his proposal because he wanted her—he had developed feelings for her.

During the spring night before they were to leave, crazy thoughts whirled around in her head—she couldn't sleep, sipping coffee from her old cracked mug at the table all night, trying to convince herself that what she was about to do, sinful for sure, was her chance for happiness. Jonas had just celebrated his eighteenth birthday—he was an adult now—hopefully he'd find a wife, have a family, and survive without his mother's constant presence. She looked around the room, and then walked to the window to watch the sun rise, still sipping from the mug she clutched in both hands.

She went to the bedroom, packed one bag, and sat on the porch swing wearing her frayed, secondhand sweater and matching stocking cap, and waited until Fritz came in from doing the morning chores. "I'm leaving you, and I don't wanna argue or fight. I'm just leaving." Fritz became enraged and began shouting, then started to go inside for his shotgun but stopped short of opening the door. "I'll kill you before I let you leave, you have a husband and a son!" His warnings were becoming yells, finally a scream. "Who in the hell do you think you are, some kind of goddamn princess? You're an ugly-looking old bag with no brains, who the hell is gonna take care of you?" She stayed calm. "If you touch me now, or ever again, I'll call the police and have you arrested." She refused to engage in the shouting—raising her head defiantly, and as tears welled up in her eyes, then flowing down her cheeks, she said, "I don't have to take abuse from you or anyone else, and I'm not gonna!" It took courage, but she walked away, out the lane to Mexico Road, and then the two miles to the man's house just as he was leaving for his last day on the job. He smiled broadly when he saw her standing by his car holding her bag. He would've come for her, but she had insisted he not, she needed to walk away—leave by herself, not allow Fritz to blame another man for taking his wife away.

Jonas never forgave his mother for leaving. When she returned to visit after Fritz's death, he wouldn't answer the door. He never allowed her inside the house.

In the fall of 1937, around the same time Will left for West Point, Fritz began to speak out and write about Adolph Hitler leading Germany out of the depth of economic depression resulting from the sanctions imposed by the international community after World War I. At the same time the German army was rallying behind the Nazi party, winning battle after battle and conquering territory.

He also praised Hitler's plan to develop a superior Aryan race. Two years earlier, in 1935, Fritz had begun inviting dangerous people to the farm, playing host to meetings of various Nazi organizations and white supremacist groups. Ku Klux Klan members held rallies while wearing their notorious white sheets—their flaming crosses sharing the fields with Fritz's corn and soybeans. These meetings became more frequent in 1940 after the Klan joined with the German-American Bund, an organization financed partly by the Nazi German government, that held a large rally in New Jersey that same year. Fritz began holding more rallies and retreats at the farm, all the while Jonas was becoming deeply involved. Automobiles with license plates from many different states were seen parked at local businesses in Alton Manor, roaming the blacktop roads, or meandering up and down Mexico Road. The neighborhood's indifference was still allowing them to openly conduct their meetings, rallies, and cross burnings, the obsession with privacy the excuse for apathy and silence.

Fritz raised money for the party and invited German Nazi officials to America as his guests, paying all their travel expenses, and flaunted the influence he claimed to have by arranging for supporters to meet the Germans. These supporters wanted to be part of the movement, offering their services, hoping to gain favor for themselves, especially as world domination was thought possible. The justice and treasury departments launched investigations and the IRS audited him, looking for evidence of money laundering, stolen guns, illegal gun sales, and tax evasion, but nothing illegal or irregular was found.

He began surrounding himself with a small group of trusted aides, and put Jonas in charge of recruiting and training soldiers. Ben and Hannah Kaiser, a young married couple in their early thirties from New Jersey, moved to the farm. Ben was arrogant, hurling insults and sarcasms at people accompanied by a mocking grin. He wore his sandy brown hair in crew-cut style with a little on top of his balding head, his high hairline creating a big round face with wide-open blue eyes and thick eyebrows and lips. During the summer he was always tanned from working outdoors. Hannah was a petite woman—she wore her blond hair in a ponytail. Her face was undistinguishable except for an occasional blemish and acne scar. Her blue eyes, subtle smile, and quiet voice accentuated her pleasant and gentle personality. Hannah, not good at cooking or keeping house, began helping Jonas at the farmer's market in Alton Manor— he had opened a booth selling guns, ammunition, and World War I souvenirs.

The farmer's market, still in operation, consists of three whitewashed concrete block buildings with shingled roofs. These buildings replaced old dilapidated wooden ones demolished over forty years earlier. Landscaping has a low priority—there isn't anything fancy about this place. Sparsely scattered weeds, about a foot or two tall, green in summer, brown and brittle during winter, stand up along the buildings, hiding the empty soda cans, beer bottles, and paper and plastic litter thrown on the ground despite the trash barrels sitting all about. The main building is about three hundred feet long with a few windows, and about sixty feet wide, with double doors at each end—additional doors are on both sides. The merchant's booths are lined up on both sides of two aisles. This main building is the most popular. Here are butchers, poultry farmers, and seafood jobbers selling quality foods, also featured are produce farmers, bakers, candy makers, and other merchants selling groceries, beauty aids, work clothing, plus antique and collectable dealers like Jonas. Guess your weight barkers doing their hustling and strongmen selling cure-all potions add a carnival atmosphere. During the summer, outside in the field next to the parking lot, farmers sell fruits and vegetables off the tailgates of their trucks, and auctioneers hawk their junk goods while hundreds of flea market dealers set up tables. There are also two smaller buildings, one on each side of the main building. One features farm equipment and lawn and garden tractor dealers, and furniture and home-appliance retailers use the other.

Scattered throughout the buildings are food and snack booths featuring good-tasting fare such as French fries, hot dogs, hamburgers, ice cream, and cotton candy. The smell of deep-fried fish sandwiches permeate everyone's hair and clothing, overwhelming the main building's air, unevenly heated during the winter cold—hot air blowing in your face from loud wall mounted heaters, never reaching below the knees, so your legs and feet are always cold. In summer the buildings are sticky and humid, hardly any air moves. People shop and then escape to the picnic tables scattered around the market grounds, eating, smoking, chatting, or just relaxing while listening to various bands performing on a small stage in the courtyard. The market attracts locals and tourists—a few thousand people show up every day. Rufus and Alvin Labe, two old brothers owned it back then, they inherited it from their father. Members of the Labe family still own it—it remains the center of activity for the Alton Manor community.

Rudolf Hammerschmidt, an accomplished gunsmith, showed up at the Konrad farm one day to join the movement. "I'm willing to do anything that'll help the cause." He was a large man in his mid thirties, not fat—huge hands and feet, a face puffy, almost like a prizefighter's, and a crew cut. He was at least 6' 3" tall and weighed 300 pounds—all muscle. A bachelor, he worked as a security guard at various warehouses in Rossville, stealing merchandise every opportunity he got. He had met Jonas at the market booth, sold him three rifles and a handgun he had stolen. He moved to the Konrad farm, was given room and board, and was put in charge of security.

Alfred Shrum and Sophia Hummel, middle-age lovers who rode on Alfred's motorcycle attending racist rallies and looking for any opportunity to engage in street fighting, were invited to the farm after Jonas met them at a Klan rally in Maryland. Alfred was an unemployed auto mechanic who chain-smoked unfiltered cigarettes. He was short and overweight, with a fat neck and bulbous nose full of busted blood vessels from years of alcohol abuse. His face, he kept it clean-shaven, featured deep acne scars and a reddish complexion from all the tiny broken capillaries. He wore his long greasy hair in a ponytail, dyed black—like boot polish, fake looking from repeated overdoing of dye and peroxide. He always wore denim with a white T-shirt, black leather boots and gold chains around his neck, and seldom carried a gun.

"I don't need any guns, man, I've got my baseball bat." He liked to tell people how tough he was. "Sophia lures these ignorant niggers away from their crowd, and I catch 'em off guard when they're standing there talking to her, thinking they're gonna get a piece of white ass. I sneak up from behind and do a homerun swing across their legs, breaking as many bones as I can—if I have time I give 'em a second whack!" Sophia gleefully boasted, "This fucker enjoys hearing 'em moan as we run to the bike and roar away!"

Sophia, five years younger than Alfred, was slightly overweight over the buttocks. She had a pretty face, was attractive in a natural way—she never wore makeup, her long dark brown hair hanging straight. She dressed in halter-tops, tight jeans, sandals, and during the winter, the leather jacket that Alfred bought her. She was violent—her bad temper got her into many barroom fights with other women. She'd usually fight them with a knife, which she wasn't afraid to use on women or men. All the assaults she was arrested for were stabbings.

Fritz gave Alfred the job of organizing disruptions at war bond rallies and other gatherings supporting the American war effort. Sophia helped take care of the farmhouse, cleaning, cooking, and doing the laundry.

One night Jonas was awakened to find Sophia cuddled up against him, asleep. Startled, but not wanting to awaken her, he fell back asleep and then awoke in the morning to the sound of her singing loudly—she was naked in the bathtub. "Are you gonna ask me to come back to bed?" He was all set to confess he had no experience at sex but kept quiet, anxious for the chance to take advantage of whatever she offered. He nodded while keeping his eyes riveted on her. She started to sing again—softly now—and then stood up slowly, flattered by his obvious joy looking at her, she made sure he saw everything.

He was surprised he was so enduring—his first time. She told him it was the first time she had an orgasm in months. "I hardly ever come when Alfred's in me—he's always in a hurry." He didn't believe anything she was saying. "Did my father send you here?" She was surprised by the question. "Don't be silly, Alfred told me to fuck you—he's hoping you tell your father." Aware that he was naïve about both sex and politics, she explained, "He thinks your father will make him his favorite because he was willing to have his girlfriend make you happy—doesn't fucking me make you happy?" Jonas lit up a cigarette without answering—he never told his father or anyone else he did it with Sophia.

A couple of weeks later she awoke him in the middle of the night, slipping out of her nightgown and climbing into bed. "Get the hell outta here, I'm a nobody around here, I can't get your boyfriend any special favors—pimping you ain't getting him anywhere." Sophia put her lips against his, then her tongue in his mouth. Snuggling under the covers, she put her left leg over him and whispered, "He doesn't know I'm here, are you gonna tell him?" He put his hand at her crotch and she began to move, getting so excited she cried out. They did it all-night—he put his hand gently over her mouth to muffle her moans and cries for more of him. They began having sex whenever Alfred was away.

Petty thieves, alcoholics, the homeless, the mentally retarded, and other misfits were constantly being recruited to be soldiers. They wondered on and off the Konrad farm, many of them only interested in the food, a warm bed, and the alcohol and drugs they could get in return for going through the political indoctrination and military drill. The ones that stayed, usually eight to twelve at any one time, became foot soldiers and were promised a future with money and power. They were charged with maintaining the large cache of arms, assisting to mail hate literature, helping to host the visiting Nazi and Klan officials, and providing security—keeping trespassers out.

Two years earlier, in 1938, the Nazis in Germany began to develop "the final solution". Hitler's regime forced the puppet governments they controlled to pass anti-Semitic laws and carrying out the extermination of the Jewish and Gypsy populations by forced labor, starvation, massacre, or systematic execution.

One evening in 1940, Fritz took his son for a long walk to talk and confide in as equals for the first time. Jonas felt uneasy because he had feared his father when he was a child, and as an adult a fear, though different, was still present inside him. He had listened to his father's fanatical speeches, helped him conduct rallies where he'd scream predictions of the end of society as presently known—that the Jews will take over American business, black children will cause the degeneration of the schools, and black men will impregnate all the white women.

It was time for Fritz to prepare a successor. "When the party takes control of this country, there's gonna be people like us put in charge of things. We'll be rewarded with power and respect. That's why we must get ready now, prepare to eliminate the enemies of society, and we'll be allowed to include the people that have harmed us personally—I've been assured of that. Will Hartman is fighting against our cause, and his family has tried to ruin me. I'm gonna kill him and burn the Oregon Inn to the ground!"

When Jonas began the transformation from pretending to be awestruck and excited to really being so, he convinced himself that if he forgot that his father had abused him, and if he erased from his memory his mother's screams and cries, he could stay and believe what his father believed.

While they walked up the farm lane, and then along Mexico Road, Fritz warned, "If you tell anyone what we're about to do here, they'll kill you." Jonas swallowed hard. "Who are 'they'?" Fritz didn't want to talk about details. "I'm 'they,' you're 'they,' all of us here on the farm are 'they,' and all members of the party and this movement are 'they'." The answer brought chilling thoughts to Jonas, but the next words from Fritz stunned him. "From this moment on I consider you my successor." They stopped walking, and for the first time in his life, Jonas embraced his father.

One early morning in the spring of 1942, Jonas watched Alfred and Rudolf unload from a rented moving van an old crematorium Fritz had bought from a scrap-iron dealer in Philadelphia for one hundred dollars. After logs were put under it, the monstrosity was pushed and dragged, then taken apart and re-assembled in the small utility house attached to the back of the main house by a short covered walkway. These type of utility houses were used by the early Pennsylvania German settlers as summer kitchens, housing a large open hearth for cooking—allowing the main house to stay cooler during the hot, humid days of summer. The summer kitchens also enabled foodstuffs to be refrigerated by submersion in the cool water springs flowing through their cellars.

The challenging task of getting the oven operational began in earnest. Valuable scrap copper and brass parts had already been removed—they had to be replaced, and because they had become obsolete a lot of improvising and reinventing needed to be done. The installation of the oven was a closely guarded secret—even American Nazi party officials were unaware of it existence. He was convinced when the American government collapsed, the extermination program would begin immediately using his crematorium, and he'd be rewarded because he had a plan ready. He had decided that installing a gas chamber could wait—until then executions would be accomplished by firing squad.

Recognizing the need to practice using the oven, Rudolf got a job guarding the county medical lab in Rossville. Using money Fritz gave him to bribe a low-paid janitor willing to look the other way, Rudolf put unclaimed cadavers in body bags and loaded them into his car's trunk, bringing them home late at night, perhaps one or two a month—within hours they were incinerated.

During the war years, Nazi and Klan activity at the farm was feverishly taking place, and Jonas's gun and souvenir business at the market had become very lucrative—he had become an accredited appraiser.

In May 1945 Jonas came in off the fields to each lunch and heard the news blaring from the large floor-model radio in the Konrad kitchen: Germany had surrendered! Stunned, he staggered to a chair and collapsed in it. Regaining his composure, he asked, "Where's my father?" Sophia, also upset by the news, came running into the room and said, "He went outside after hearing the news and chased off all the soldiers." Jonas leapt to his feet and hurried outside, frantically looking for signs of him, then ran to the neglected, rundown barn and yelled through the partially opened doors into the darkness. "Pop, the news can't be as bad as what they're reporting, the party will survive, come back to the house!"

Getting no response, he opened the doors wide—the bright rays of sunshine met the body hanging by its neck from a rafter, swinging slightly back and forth, pushed by the strong springtime breeze. Jonas watched the occasional jerking of an arm or leg—the twitching body not quite yet giving in to the tragic and dead mind. Finally with a deflating sag, it got still.

Chapter 3

Lieutenant Colonel Will Hartman, soldier, widower, and father, sat exhausted at the kitchen table in the dimly lit farmhouse in a nameless small village near Ulm, Germany. Only a few candles lit the rooms, one in particular at his table so he could read the maps and messages necessary to command. The ground in this heavily wooded area had been shaking every five seconds for over twenty hours—the loud thunder of distant shelling sent by the Allies to the Germans had begun to dull the senses, and then shocked into frenzy when a German shell landed in the lap of the Americans. He thought by now he'd have adapted, but each burst of shell harshly reminded him that he was frazzled.

It was April 24, 1945. About 11 o'clock that night the shelling stopped, but the unceasing vibration and deafening sound of the droning tanks moving along the mud road, replacing one vexation for another, seemed like a never-ending condition of life. It had been weeks now, everything sinking and staggering in the mud created by days of rain—tanks, trucks, caissons, and soldier's feet. Equipment was constantly breaking down, and the smell of spilling and splashing fuel and the exhaust fumes from the tanks and other vehicles were violating the air. The sight and sound of aircraft approaching no longer brought panic to the men. Now it was Allied aircraft providing air support, the Luftwaffe had been virtually destroyed except for a few remaining light and low-flying aircraft the desperate enemy was using for reconnaissance. Still there was trauma associated with the haunting and thunderous sound when added to the chaotic struggle for survival being played out on the ground.

The soldiers' bodies ached from miles of walking without taking any time to rest. They lacked sleep and were further fatigued because of few rations, little water to drink and none to bathe. These conditions played out the Allied movement east. The never changing orders from higher command were to keep moving and keep fighting.

Will's infantrymen had been ordered to enter villages, one by one, ridding them of sniper nests and securing weapons and ammunition and anything else of value abandoned by the retreating enemy. After the foot soldiers found and shot any snipers, they called in support troops to secure the booty. Then the tanks blew holes in buildings and ran through them and over stone fences without feeling a jerk, shaking the ground as if the planet was being jarred off its axis. Allied and enemy soldiers were being killed and wounded seemingly with ever-increasing occurrence—medics were overwhelmed as they frantically tried to care for fallen men.

Men shouting into radios, only getting static and broken responses, filled the house as others raced from one room to the other setting up battalion headquarters. The unit was ordered to establish this position and plan to be there for about forty-eight hours before continuing on. He sat at the kitchen table, left alone by his men who knew he needed some solace.

"Dear Mother," he wrote to Katie, "We're moving east in the massive effort to end this war. I'm so tired I think I would give away my soul for just four hours of undisturbed sleep." He had written her the day before, "Losing Magdalena and the exhaustion from combat is giving me an overwhelming feeling of devastation. I feel better knowing Henrietta is there to help you care for the baby and run the inn—it won't be long now and I'll be home. I cheer up a little bit when I think of that, but I know that my grief is going to be even worse when I don't have to worry about commanding men in combat. We live minute to minute, never knowing when the enemy will confront us. We're no longer being bombarded with enemy aircraft fire that traveled along the ground so fast you had no time to do anything but watch as bodies are shot to pieces. The German air force has been destroyed, but the snipers wait for us as we enter each town. It will be over soon, I keep praying that it comes in the next hour, which isn't soon enough."

The worn-out men were pitching tents or finding shelter in barns, stables, or other farm outbuildings, anywhere they could get under a roof and build small fires to get their clothes dry. The latest dose of heavy rain continued for three days, and it now poured down during the late night, a night darkened to excess by the blackout imposed to limit detection.

Will was sipping his cup of coffee when Captain Bill Ganttrano, commander of Company A, came into the house. "Sir, are there any objections to the staff killing some chickens?" Ganttrano was a short man, thirty-six years old, older than Will and the other officers because he had served before as an enlisted man. He frequently reminded young privates that he could connect to them because he entered the army as they did, part of the lowest link of the chain of command. He was constantly smoking a cigarette and used hair cream to put a shine on his black hair that he combed straight back, which called attention to his receding hairline. A shortage of officers had given him the opportunity to attend officer candidate school. The school's mission was to find men who had such a compelling wish to be officers that they were willing to endure constant mindless harassment for twenty-three weeks. With only a small amount of academic preparation, he was commissioned a second lieutenant.

He grew up in inner city Baltimore, fighting his way through high school, barely graduating. He bounced from one menial job to the next until he realized that for someone like him crime was much more lucrative. His modus operandi was walking into jewelry stores, kicking in one of the display cases and scooping up the diamond bracelets. After letting the cache cool down for a month or two, he'd go to wealthy neighborhoods and sell the goods door to door. One day he knocked on the door of the district attorney's mother while her son was visiting. Bill Ganttrano found himself with a choice, jail or the army. He knew he was getting a break, and the prosecutors knew they'd have a hard time tracing all the stolen jewelry and building a case, strongly suspecting that their investigation would lead them to the jewelry boxes of rich and powerful citizens, destinations they preferred to avoid. It just seemed a lot easier to get him out of town and into the war instead of creating political pandemonium.

Combat situations allowed his violent temper to be masqueraded as a brash style of commanding—shouting, screaming, and threatening. He had killed more enemy soldiers than anyone else in the battalion, always looking for any opportunity to lead patrols and do more killing. Will became convinced that Ganttrano was a psychopath—getting pleasure from the war, killing other human beings was mesmerizing to him. He never was really comfortable being near this repulsive man—even in the violent war environment he had to watch him a lot closer than the other commanders.

Will also found Ganttrano's lifestyle repugnant. Back in New Jersey, before deploying, he had noticed him leaving for a night out, going into the run-down army-post town outfitted with pinky rings, gold chains, low-buttoned shirt, and offensive strong-smelling cologne, which he splashed in excess on his entire hairy upper torso.

Will asked, "Whose chickens are they?" Ganttrano tried to answer all the expected questions. "The farmer told us to kill whatever we want to eat, he knows the war is almost over and is happy the Americans are here and not 'those goddamn

Russian bastards'." Will reminded him of the blackout, and then gave cautious consent.

The chaplain came to see him, and while they sat in front of the fireplace, the flames taking some of the dampness from the air, he sought to console the war-weary commander, telling what Will already knew—he must not only fight the battles of the war, but find the strength to resist being overwhelmed by personal tragedy. "God will guide you through all this if you allow him." The words seemed hollow to Will, but when the clergyman asked, he agreed to join him in prayer, asking God for renewed and continued strength and guidance.

He lied down in one of the bedrooms to get a few hours' sleep. At about two o'clock in the morning, Ganttrano knocked on the door and told him they were just radioed that General Stuckey will be coming for a meeting with the battalion commanders in about an hour. Will crawled out of bed, came into the kitchen, and was caught by surprise by one of the general's staff officers, who began a hasty briefing, an unemotional monologue. "Colonel, General Stuckey will be ordering your battalion to proceed, as the forward position force, on an alternate route to begin liberating a prisoner-of-war camp in the town of Dachau, just southeast of here. It will be a sensitive assignment, and your men will be the first Americans arriving at the camp. They must be kept under very tight control with strict orders to treat all the prisoners, military and civilian, compassionately, and prepare them for release from confinement." He handed him maps to be used during the movement, stressing that the large force following will be relying on his battalion to resume leading the main forward movement after the camp has been liberated.

Stuckey's other staff members and the battalion commanders started coming in. Everybody arose and came to attention when the general arrived, he stood over six feet tall, and the stars on his collar overwhelmed the small dining room, he carried them quite well. "Colonel Hartman, you've been briefed, do you have any questions?" Will knew he needed to keep his response short. "Sir, what do I do with the liberated prisoners?" He expected Will's very question, and gave a short and fast answer, "Tell them to go outside the fences and wait for food, medical care, and transportation." Stuckey never pondered defeat—he was an egomaniac, convinced he would always be victorious as long as his orders were followed. The general and his staff hurriedly departed into the night. Will turned to his commanders and gave his orders. "Brief your men and be ready to move out at 0500 hours."

The next day they entered Augsburg where they met up with more American troops who were to support his battalion's rear as it entered Dachau, and the next day they arrived just a few miles short of entering the camp. The advance squads soon were coming back with grisly details of what they saw. The camp wasn't a prisoner-of-war camp—it was a concentration camp, a hell on earth. A platoon sergeant, returning for more men, was stopped by Will. "We can still smell the stench of burning flesh coming from the ovens, Colonel, I never imagined that I'd ever see anything like this as long as God allowed me on this earth." A young lieutenant agonized, "What would possess men to think that they had the right to kill other people by the thousands?" Will, seeing the young officer was shaken, encouraged him to talk. "It's bad enough they killed men, and worse yet, women, but to kill little, defenseless children, making mothers choose which of their children must go to the gas chamber, and if they refused, sending them all, is beyond my ability to comprehend."

As the battalion of liberators was entering the area, the Nazi guards were surrendering, giving no armed resistance. Will prepared to enter the camp to assist in the arrest of the camp commandant and his staff.

Now he saw the unspeakable horrors firsthand. Men can become used to just about anything when exposed to it long enough. One supposes that if you find yourself living in hell, then hell will eventually become the norm. For a sane person, exposure to such genocide, especially so abruptly, is extremely distressing—it was especially trying to Will's fragile state of mind. Regardless, as an army officer he had to perform his mission in an efficient, systematic manner, all the while quietly maintaining his composure.

He began interrogating prisoners and captured Nazi officers. They told him thousands of people were forced to watch as their invalid parents were hauled off to the gas chamber, old and defenseless, they had worked all of their lives, only to die bankrupt, everything they ever owned confiscated. Men, who had all their dreams destroyed, watched as the camp guards murdered their children and grandchildren, and their wives and daughters put to death after being raped by the SS soldiers. All this until it was their turn to be gassed. The Nazis had decided to butcher millions of people they considered subhuman, their lives a wasted absurd existence.

Before it was their turn to die, women were forced to work as cooks, housecleaners, laundry workers, and mistresses for the camp officers. The men dug the mass graves, sorted the clothing, jewelry, and other meager possessions of the dead. They mended the fences, repaired roofs, laboring from sun up until sun down. They were gassed when new workers less starved arrived.

Will and his men moved swiftly through the camp, securing building after building, opening gates, assisting the delicate, tragic living skeletons, showing them the way to the outside. They performed the tasks in somber silence.

He thought, to a certain extent instinctively, having Ganttrano by his side might help him get through the ordeal because he was insensitive and devoid of feelings for other human beings. "You know, Stuckey knew what he was sending us to do, he should have warned me, I still could've accomplished the mission, but I would've been better prepared." Ganttrano countered, "I couldn't care less. I just do what they tell me to do." He was reacting just the way Will expected. "If I was you I wouldn't worry so much about any of this bullshit, soon we'll be out of here forever." At that particular time, for just a few hours, Will felt he needed to be with someone callous enough to counteract the nightmare his men were living through—that someone was Captain Bill Ganttrano.

The battalion search crew, carrying out a methodical room-by-room search, came across the quarters of SS officer Hermann Vogelweh, a deputy camp commandant. Will and a squad, including Ganttrano, entered and found the Nazi standing with his hands raised, frantically muttering in German, his assistant anxiously raising his too after dropping a pistol.

Ganttrano, shouting, asked if either could speak English—neither responded. He handcuffed their hands behind them and shoved them onto the office couch. "Somebody go get some MPs and an interpreter to translate Colonel Hartman's interrogation." Will told the rest of the squad, "Continue the search, Captain Ganttrano and I will catch up after I question these two." He ordered a sergeant posted outside the door until the MPs returned. Ganttrano saw yet another opportunity to kill the enemy. "Sir, let's save ourselves a lot of work, let's execute the mother fuckers, you know they're gonna get away with murder if we take 'em prisoner." Will ignored the suggestion. "Search them and check for any valuables or papers." Ganttrano wasn't gentle while rifling their pockets. "Look what I found Colonel, the 'easy-way-out pill' that these perverted bastards use to kill themselves." Holding the pill between his thumb and forefinger and putting his pistol against the assistant's head with his other hand, he yelled, "Here's your choice, you sick son of a bitch, take the pill or take a bullet." Disorder was everywhere—soldiers could be heard running up and down the hallway responding to the sporadic gunfire outside. Will shouted for him to stop, but before he could react further, Ganttrano dropped the pill into the Nazi's mouth, his tongue pulling the pill in like a bug-catching frog's, his destiny now settled. At the same time, Vogelweh, in the blink of an eye, slithered off the couch, fell to his knees, and veered his head to the end table where his suicide pill had been laid. His tongue flailed out like a rattlesnake's, getting the pill in his belly lickety-split. Will grabbed him by his hair, violently jerking his head away from the table, then dragging him across the floor. The assistant, passed out, was well on his way to hell, Vogelweh was already beginning his journey, gagging and twitching from the poison pill's effects.

Will had lost control, failing as an officer. Ganttrano was flawed, probably as bad as the Nazis, but Will was the commander—a West Pointer, disciplined to act decisively in time of crisis, to function superbly under awesome pressure, and to accept responsibility for the actions of each of his men.

He considered bringing charges, having Ganttrano court-martialed for murdering the assistant. How would he explain Vogelweh's suicide? Will was convinced a military court, in time of war, never would convict Ganttrano. He'd lie, testify that the assistant grabbed the pill and placed it in his mouth, and he'd tell the court his superior officer couldn't have possibly witnessed it because he was struggling with Vogelweh. Will knew there's always a price to pay for having people like Bill Ganttrano members of your command, people who under the cover of war indulge in murder and rape.

The battalion's mission accomplished, Will ordered his men out of the camp. His official report stated Vogelweh and his assistant committed suicide, each swallowing a suicide pill just as his quarters were entered, a story different from what actually happened. Following the Hartman tradition of holding yourself to very high standards, sometimes exceeding the bounds of reason, he would never again be able to judge his military service as honorable, notwithstanding what the official record showed. He violated his oath and disgraced his uniform, failing to be in control during chaos. Ganttrano knew the truth, but his lack of self-respect and a moral code allowed him to easily live with the deceit.

The following day, after setting up camp in a field twenty miles away, Ganttrano went to Will's tent to discuss the events of the previous day. "Colonel, I've always tried to do what they sent me here to do, kill Nazis." Will wasn't in the mood for him. "We're supposed to take prisoners—that's one of the rules of war—not to become what they are." Ganttrano snarled back, "To hell with the rules of war. Your report is what the official record says happened, you wrote it, and I ain't telling anybody that you're a liar, sir, and that's my fuckin rule of war."

Chapter 4

The bus full of sweaty passengers, Will Hartman was one of them, pulled up to the Rossville bus station on a hot and humid July day in 1945. Will was back stateside, released from active duty. Keeping it secret, he had requested admittance to a veteran's psychiatric hospital—the physician giving him is discharge physical observed symptoms of battle fatigue and made the referral. Grief from losing Magdalena, and guilt from his perceived failing as an officer intensified when combat ended.

The hospital was forty miles away from Rossville. Two times a week, usually on a weekday, and then again on Sundays, Henrietta would drive there to visit and Katie would hold Seth. When he napped, she laid him on a pretty blue blanket on the back seat, fanning him with one of the fold up Chinese fans sold to the inn's guests. They'd all be sweaty by the time they got there, the hot summer air rushing in the open car windows making their faces blushed and hair wind blown.

Will underwent a schedule of intense therapy, the psychiatrists and psychologists knew his depression was a result of losing his wife—they felt he would eventually be able to rationalize the stressful circumstances at Dachau. During therapy he described the Hartman men that came before him and how they were respected by their families and the community. Hard work and shrewd business practices, commitment to their wives and children enabled them to carry on the family's legacy. He told the doctors he always wanted to live a life like each of those Hartmans, happy and prosperous with virtue. Now he was questioning whether that was possible.

Responding to therapy would be slow—a long journey was ahead of him. He had no wife. He had no military career, no farm to make productive, and he was too ill to raise the son he fathered. All that contradicted the lives of those Hartman men of the past.

After six months, just when his treatment was beginning to show progress, he was prescribed medication, scheduled for regular outpatient therapy, and discharged. The hospital administration's decision, made necessary by critical overcrowding, took away the time Will needed to heal. Sent on his way, Will found comfort drinking heavily and taking prescription drugs—failed life preservers in a giant sea of self-pity.

The local folks back home, unaware of his mental state and his increasing alcohol and drug use, gave their hometown boy a hero's reception. The newspaper and radio station declared this 'young, handsome West Point graduate', who helped 'rescue Europe' and liberate the concentration camp in Dachau, a 'champion of freedom'. He was gracious while receiving all these accolades, attending award ceremonies, being the guest of honor at banquets, giving speeches to local civic and church groups, and addressing the student body of the high school that only a few years earlier he was attending as a lanky-limbed adolescent.

But behind the mask he wore to portray the appreciative honored patriot, Will Hartman, the mourning widower and secretly ashamed army officer, also had to deal with an additional serious problem. His family's country inn was about to go bankrupt. He kept drinking despite recalling his father's advice years ago; "The first thing you do if you have a drinking

MEXICO ROAD | 51

problem is sell the goddamn liquor license." People began to notice—instead of being the pleasant and friendly man they knew since he was a kid—he was becoming quiet and withdrawn. He spent most days and nights sitting at the bar making sure nobody walked off with the place.

His mother was concerned. Katie's dark brown hair was starting to see some gray ones, and the lenses on her trademark pink plastic frames were thicker now, but she was still healthy and spry, but wanting to slow down—she had run the inn practically single handedly for many years. She had always been hardworking, accepting more than her share of responsibilities, continuing to do most of the inn's cooking and helping care for Seth, who was destined to become increasingly dependent and devoted to his grandmother.

She never wished Will to be the next innkeeper, she had wanted him to be an army officer, maybe later a civil engineer, but circumstances can force people to change the direction of their lives, sometimes even whole families. The Oregon Inn is where Will belonged now, and Katie, accepting that, wanted him to get well, take his turn and take over.

She went to his room every morning before coming downstairs, trying to help him overcome his depression. "Will, life must go on, you've got to be brave and face the challenges. You need to stop drinking, alcohol will only make your problems worse." She rubbed his hand between both of hers, revealing her own anguish as well. "My heart aches for you, I gave birth to you, and I grieve when you grieve."

He looked up at her—a look of despair. "Mother, I lost my wife, and in just a few seconds I ruined my military career because I wasn't responsible." Sitting up now, he mustered enough physical strength, worn down by medication and dejection, to explain how he felt. "I've come home to my son, who has an entire life ahead of him, and I feel so exhausted I just can't reach down inside of me to be his father." Katie held out her arms, and he leaned his head into her bosom, "I feel like a child when I burden you like this," he apologized. "I'll be here for you as long as it takes for you to sort things out, continue to see your doctors, take your medication, and try not to be so tough on yourself." She knew it was hard to help someone deal with the horrors of war without having the experience. "I wasn't there, but I know you and your men were under terrible stress, you were tired, and if you made some wrong decisions, other officers would have made the same mistakes, you've got to overcome this."

The following year he did stop drinking. The medication was helping treat his depression, but keeping him in a perpetual foggy state of mind. He continued to see a therapist once a week. Henrietta would drive him to Rossville and from there he'd take the bus the forty miles or so to the clinic.

In fall, 1948, not seeing his former commander for over three years, former captain Bill Ganttrano walked into the Oregon Inn. Will didn't know what to say, so he just stared at him. He slid on to the barstool cautiously as if taking someone else's seat. "I went back to Baltimore to look up my old friends, but then I remembered I didn't have any." Reacting to that 'joke' by flashing a broad smile, immediately replaced with an uneasy one—he took time to light up a cigarette. "Will I need a job, and I really think I can help you get things straightened out around here." It had taken him a month to build up enough courage to come. "I know I'm not one of your favorite people, but I heard you're having a hard time—you're gonna need somebody to run this place until you get your shit together." Will had kept staring at him, but finally said, "You remind me of everything I'm trying to forget, why would I want you here?" The fast talker had just the answer Will needed to hear. "When we captured Dachau you said you wanted me near you because I don't give a shit about anybody or anything, and that's what got you through it." He was giving Will the biggest sales pitch he ever gave to anybody. "It's not that I don't care, it's that I just don't let it bother me." He was lying. He really didn't care. He had been hanging around the area for a couple days, mustering enough backbone to finally show up at the inn. "People in Alton Manor told me you're about ready to lose your ass here, this place is losing money every day. I stopped at a bar and two guys told me the bank's gonna foreclose on you. The whole town's worried about you and your family." He was playing the role of concerned friend—actually just trying to get Will to raise his opinion of him. "I'll do whatever it takes to make this place a moneymaking operation again. That's gonna take balls, that's gonna take somebody that don't take any shit from anybody and can relate to the men who come here spending money to drink, men we need to get in here. I'm one of 'em."

After Will explained his mother and sister-in-law are doing a good job of running the place and caring for his son, Bill began hammering away again. "Will, running a hotel is a rough business, you need a man to negotiate the best prices from suppliers, there are more trouble makers now, you need a man to keep 'em out, you need a man to schedule and take care of the maintenance, I can keep all these things under control." He stood up and looked around the barroom. "If your mother and sister-in-law are doing such a terrific job with this place, how come the paint is peeling, windows are cracked, and there are more than a few rotten boards on the porch? The shingles on the roof don't look very good—it looks to me like there ain't any money to maintain the place, and that means sure disaster is just a few years or months." Will, looking across the room at a bucket strategically placed to catch dripping rainwater from the leaking roof coming through the room upstairs, was unable to disagree with him. Bill kept up the barrage. "Colonel, I grew up on the streets of Baltimore, I've been hanging in bars since I was sixteen years old. I know how to make money with a bar. Let me help here, let's help each other."

Ganttrano noticed that drugs were making a marked difference in Will. "It was unfortunate what happened to us over there, but time will sort it all out in your mind. Let me tell you something—if I'd walked into Vogelweh's quarters alone, reasonably sure there wouldn't have been any witnesses, I would've blew both there heads off. I don't think about what happened that day, I think about what could've happened."

Will, admitting a lot of what Bill was saying made sense, decided to help out his errant army comrade. "You can stay here and help my mother and Henrietta run the place, maybe you can save it." He didn't want him to feel over welcomed. "You can have a room, food, and I'll give you a few bucks a week."

Will was desperate, fooling himself into believing there actually was a chance Ganttrano's arrogance could rescue the inn, and that nothing more could be lost by employing him. At first Bill was glad just to have a bed and some food, but after a week of playing big shot and bossing the help around, he realized he could use his criminal expertise to make a lot of money. The young punks he knew in Baltimore who made up a new generation of thugs, no longer robbing jewelry stores, were making big money drug dealing. He was convinced that the locals living near the Oregon Inn would give him plenty of business.

When Will told Katie and Henrietta he hired Ganttrano as manager Henrietta didn't say much, she let Katie do the talking. "This place has always been run by Hartmans, I'll do what you say, but I want you to get straightened out and take back the job as innkeeper." Will was willing to tell the two women anything to get them to cooperate, giving him the opportunity to hand the work and responsibility over to anybody, even Bill Ganttrano. "Mother, I promise you I will, just give me a little time." He was in no hurry.

A few nights later Katie, resting upstairs in her room, suddenly heard loud music and men cheering and applauding. Curious to find out what all the commotion was about, she walked down the hall and asked Henrietta, who was coming up the stairs after satisfying her own curiosity, "What in God's name is going on down there?" Henrietta answered, "We have a disk jockey, two naked dancers, and about a hundred men drinking and raising hell—they're buying beer faster than they can serve it!" Katie spun around and went to Will's room, walking in without knocking. Sleeping in his chair, she shook him awake. "Will, do you know what's going on downstairs?" He looked up—his glassy and squinting gray eyes revealing a heavy drug influence. "Yea I know, Bill's getting the bank paid."

Henrietta followed Katie into the room and was alarmed when she saw Will. "What pills did you take—who gave them to you? You look terrible!" Will was mumbling, his head bobbing around, barely able to speak. "Bill got me some other pills today, he said they'd help me more than the clinic's." Katie, visibly shaken, asked Henrietta, "What should we do?" Henrietta shrugged her shoulders.

Katie distrusted Ganttrano from the moment she met him, she had always used an intuition to judge character. She could tell he was a violent and unpredictable man. Will had told her about his past, describing him as a former "street smart hoodlum" who had a bad childhood. She was convinced his scandalous past was a prelude to the career of crime he was surely planning. In any case, she knew she might have to compromise on some issues facing the inn for the sake of saving it from closing—holding out the hope that it'll stay in Will and Seth's future.

Early one weekday morning, with only a few dining room tables occupied by people having breakfast, the staff was preparing to open up the barroom for another day. A truck driver delivering kegs of beer, noticing Will sitting at the end of the bar as usual, asked if he wanted to put a new lager on tap. "See if the drinkers like the taste of it." Will started to reply, but Ganttrano walked in and interrupted. "Hey, I'm Bill Ganttrano, I'm the manager here now, from now on you deal with me and only me." The driver, taken aback, nodded his head as he glanced toward Will. Ganttrano continued, "Don't look at him, you heard what I said, finish up delivering and get your ass outta here, we're not trying anything new right now."

He was attracted to Henrietta, flirting with her, giving her his signature phony smile while making suggestive comments. She gave him no encouragement—mostly ignoring him—she disliked his overconfident and abrasive personality. She didn't like his looks, she liked tall men, he was short. She told Katie, "That cologne he wears is so strong it burns my eyes, it smells like cat piss." He couldn't take the hint, wasting little time pursuing her. He couldn't be blamed for wanting her—many men wanted her. She was a good-looking woman, petite, short black hair surrounding her pretty face.

When she answered his uninvited knock on the door of her second floor room, he asked, "Let's go have a few drinks at that little bar in Alton Manor, we can get to know each other." She couldn't hold back her laughter as she looked at the pathetic little man with greased-back hair standing in the hallway. "Are you asking me to have an affair with you?" He was surprised at her candor. "Well, now that you brought it up, I gotta admit it's something that crossed my mind." She laughed again, and then abruptly turned very serious. "If Sal ever found out that you asked me out, he'd have you put in the hospital, and believe me I'm not just talking." Raising his arm to hit her with the back of his hand, he paused—she didn't flinch. "You're lucky you came to your senses just in time." Her face grimaced with hate that shocked even him. "I'm gonna warn you only once," she growled, speaking very slowly, "I can have you hurt bad, you really don't want me to hate your guts any more than I already do, take my warning seriously." Her stare with such firebrand contempt dissolved any desire he had for her. He took a long drag of his cigarette, turning his head slightly to keep the exhaled smoke out of her face. He gave her another glance before turning and walking down the hall. Bill Ganttrano was quickly finding out whom he could intimidate and whom he couldn't.

Henrietta had phoned Sal to tell him Will hired his old army buddy. Sal met Ganttrano for the first time when he came to the inn a couple of weeks later on a Friday afternoon to spend the weekend. Henrietta always did what Sal told her to do—keep the books, keep her eyes and ears open, and tell him every detail of the goings-on at the inn, and now he told her to especially watch Bill Ganttrano.

Talking while having dinner, she told him what she was coping with every day. "He's so repulsive, I don't know if I can keep forcing myself to be around him. He thinks he's gonna get to keep all the money made here." She was trying to convince Sal to get rid of him. "He comes on to me, he thinks he's a lady's man." Sal started laughing. "Well he'd certainly have his hands full taking care of the wildcat in you!" He leaned over to give her a kiss, but she pulled her head away, not amused by his lack of concern—perhaps if Bill Ganttrano was handsome and a gentleman, he'd be worried about his wife being propositioned.

The financial condition of the inn continued to deteriorate. Bill was the boss for three months and the money crisis was getting worse. He had demonstrated absolutely no fiscal responsibility—Henrietta continued to struggle to pay the bills. Sal told her, "I'm gonna be forced to set up some operations here, if I don't the place will have to be shut down." She knew what that meant—gambling and prostitution. She wondered what Will was going to say. Sal said, "He ain't gonna say nothing, we're not gonna discuss it with him, he doesn't wanna be involved, so we'll make sure he's not, you just make sure he takes his pills every day." Sal knew he had to keep Ganttrano on as manager—but he planned to bring in his own people to run the illegal operations. "You're gonna stay living here, help Katie take care of Will and Seth, and make sure Ganttrano doesn't steal any of my fuckin money."

On Monday afternoon he came back from Rossville with twenty-five thousand dollars to pay all the bills current.

Henrietta pleaded again with Sal to get rid of Ganttrano—it was testing Sal's patience. "Ganttrano's a necessary evil we need to keep around to enforce the rules and become the scapegoat if anything goes wrong. He can sell his drugs, I don't care what he does as long as it doesn't cut into what I'm doing."

Sal and Bill sat at a table in the corner of the dining room. "My brother-in-law made you the manager of this place, but I'm the guy you're working for now. You can be the manager, and you can make money for yourself as long as you don't get greedy and try to steal from me." Ganttrano, displaying a rare show of respect, listened and kept his mouth shut. "And another thing, don't ever come on to my wife again. If you do, I'll have your bones broke." Sal was making sure Ganttrano understood the way the Oregon Inn was going to be run from now on. "Henrietta handles all the money except what you make on your own. You enforce my rules, making sure that every dime made here goes through her. If I ever catch you or anybody else skimming, I'll hold you responsible—then you're a fuckin dead man. Do you understand?" Ganttrano understood very well. "Sal, I'm not gonna cause you any problems." He took Sal Messaro very seriously.

Sal ordered Henrietta to evict all the tenants who were renting upstairs rooms. Eva Harrison, a big overweight woman from New Jersey, showed up with five prostitutes, and Big John Weldon, a huge and tall black man from New York, also overweight, started running high-stakes poker games in a back room down in the inn's cellar. Many of Sal's cronies, all involved in various rackets such as hiding fugitives, loan sharking, illegal drug distribution, selling and receiving stolen property, and hiding and renaming racehorses out back in the barn, were all accommodated at the inn. Sal got a cut from everybody and everything, he was making a lot of money for himself while making sure Henrietta had enough to pay all the bills. Once a week his accountant came and doctored the inn's books—making fabricated entries.

Chapter 5

In 1950 Seth entered first grade—excited about starting school, he'd sit at a table in the inn's dining room each evening doing his homework and practicing reading. He was growing faster than suited the people who loved him, he was a good looking kid, his olive skinned complexion, black curly hair and dark eyes, bespoke his Italian mother's genes, but his facial features were the result of his German father's—high cheekbones, a straight nose and firm sturdy chin.

The new decade brought another war, television, faster cars, and a bevy of new household gadgets. Katie watched with despair at the changing atmosphere at the inn, people of questionable character moving in. She held on, protecting her sick son and growing grandson, determined the inn remain in the Hartman family—she dared not say it, but thought many times, there wasn't a price too high to pay for that.

Katie and Henrietta had become close friends because they were both committed to raising Seth. Katie was a wise woman who had seen much in her life and ran the inn almost single-handedly in another era. She knew Sal was immoral, but had to admit he also had a noble reason for grabbing control of the inn, he had been very fond of his sister-in-law—he too wanted to help provide for her son. Naturally, Henrietta's loyalty was to her husband, but Katie was comforted knowing Henrietta loved her nephew as her own.

Sal was born into a crime family, never able to separate himself from that way of life. Katie lacked an understanding of Henrietta's tolerance, most likely because of the different ethnic, religious, and cultural backgrounds—she was told Henrietta could've had almost any man she wanted—she was a beautiful woman. Men fawned over her, they still did, and a few times she was tempted, but she stayed loyal to Sal because she loved him. Her greatest sin was overlooking his crimes, ignoring the details, which Katie was convinced were horrible.

1956 came, Seth was now in sixth grade, often mischievous at this age—he liked teasing the two women—a child psychologist might say that losing his mother gave him reason to test their patience. His father was there, but Will wasn't able to give his son any emotional presence. Often while baking, Katie had to shoo him out of the kitchen. He was getting in her way and asking silly questions while waiting for warm cookies due out of the oven. Then she finally had enough. "Go outside and enjoy the woods, get some fresh air in your lungs!"

After Will quit drinking, he spent little time in the barroom, instead sleeping late, taking pills—the doctor's and Bill's, walking into Alton Manor and back, then it was more pills and more sleep. Day after day this was his routine except for the days he went to see his therapist, or when he had an anxiety attack that caused him to spend two or three weeks in the hospital.

Tension between Katie and Henrietta was rare, it happened when Henrietta mentioned Seth's religious education—Katie knew that was going to be brought up sooner or later. Henrietta said, "You know, Maggie often talked about her kids being raised as good Catholics."

Katie was careful responding—she could've used Will's support and encouragement while dealing with this issue. She didn't want to cause any riffs—Seth would be the one to suffer from that. "He should have been baptized before he was a year old, but I think Will should do that when he gets well." Henrietta said, "Katie, he's twelve years old, we're gonna have to do it, we're gonna have to agree on something."

The next morning Katie phoned the Lutheran minister at St. Paul's church, the church long supported by the Hartmans. That afternoon after he got out of school, Seth was baptized in the Lutheran faith, and arrangements were made for him to take instruction for church confirmation.

She told Henrietta what she did, and apologized for doing it without telling her first. "Forgive me, I did it this way because I didn't want us to have a confrontation." Henrietta listened, a look of resignation on her face. Katie said, "The Hartmans are Lutherans, and Seth is a Hartman."

Katie felt better now that the inn wasn't having money problems, but her other worries hadn't abated. Sitting in the dining room with Seth, she talked to him quietly, turning her head and perusing the room, making sure nobody was close enough to overhear. Ganttrano was easing her out—no longer wanting her help—he considered her a threat. She instructed, "Always keep in mind your father isn't well, he was hurt inside his head because of the terrible things he saw in the war." She didn't want to alarm the boy, but she wanted him to know there was an element of danger present. "Some of the people who say they're here to help your father are really his enemies, here only to help themselves and see what they can get out of it. You're gonna have to forget a lot of things you see and hear, it's unavoidable as long as your father is disabled or until you're old enough to take over this place."

He said, "Grandma, I know there's bad people around here, when I'm old enough to help my dad, I'm throwing 'em all the hell outta here!" She didn't like what she heard. "Don't try to be a roughneck and don't use that language, you're talking just like the thugs you want outta here," she scolded. "Learn in school, become smart, and make sure you keep the inn in the hands of Hartmans. You're fourteen years old, first you have to grow up." Ever aware of her own mortality, but still being careful not to alarm him, she urged in a firm voice, "I want you to always listen to your Aunt Henrietta, you can depend on her because she loves you very much. Sometimes she has to help the bad men, and someday you'll understand why she does the things she does."

It was easy to think Seth lucky to be growing up at a country inn. Truthfully, growing up there meant having a life full of conflict. The Oregon Inn had long ago lost its prestige clientele—it had become a crime center with behavior taking place that children normally aren't exposed to.

It was spring 1958. Katie often sat with Seth at one of the redwood tables in the inn's wooded picnic grove while he read more of Sarah Hartman's diary and looked at old family photographs she kept in a large cardboard box. She read him poetry and interesting passages from various books—starting that when he was very young—teaching him manners and proper etiquette, and demanding he maintain top grades in school and to excel in sports. She told him when his father gets well he'll be proud of him. Seth always had the same reaction when she told him that, haunting to her, he'd fix a penetrating look deep into her eyes searching for any slight hint of uneasiness in her mind when she made that revelation. She tried to give him what he could never get from his dead mother—love and guidance

In the fall he started junior high school. Rock 'n' roll music was blaring from most radios and on the inn's jukebox, Seth and his schoolmates were all wearing the current youth styles— tight pants, black loafer shoes with white swirling pleats, shirts partly unbuttoned with rolled-up high sleeves, and slicked hair combed into a ducktail, a pompadour atop their foreheads. The girls dressed in ultra-high hemmed mini-skirts, bedecking their teased up and lacquered hair with hair bands and ribbons to match their hot pink lipstick.

Maturing, he began watching more closely the men coming to the inn at the end of the workday, with sweat still on their brows, to quench their thirsts with ice-cold beer. When their children got married, most of the wedding receptions were held in the inn's dining room where enormous amounts of food and countless pitchers of beer were consumed. The Oregon Inn, despite its slide into corruption not yet noticed by most people, was still the most popular place for large family celebrations because of its dining room, the largest in the area, and Katie and Henrietta's cooking. Seth could feel the old dance floor heave up and down as the hoe-downers tortured it doing the traditional dancing to the country music—the violin's strings loosened, going from the high-pitched soft sound to the scratching tone of the fiddle.

On Friday and Saturday nights the bands played rock 'n' roll, living through the early period when it wasn't part of the main, fresh and revolutionary, all set to change the culture of the Western world. The inn's dances, just like thousands of other small grass roots venues, featured bands made up of young players dreaming of a hit record launching them to stardom and wealth.

The dances served as Seth's first exposure to the courting practices of adults. He'd sneak down the staircase and peek through the wood railing to watch couples sitting at the tables, flirting, holding hands, and kissing. He'd watch them slow-dance to the love ballads, holding and rubbing each other, then jitterbug, laughing and being wild eyed. He learned that being in love was an enviable experience—he already learned that love came in different forms, love celebrated for all the right reasons, and love prompted by lust. Some couples weren't supposed to be there together, causing irate wives to phone or come by looking for their husbands. Many would find them at a corner table with the 'other woman', or wagering their paychecks in the infamous card game, or maybe upstairs with one of the prostitutes. Terrible, violent fights broke out, men fighting men, women striking husbands or boyfriends, and occasionally two women wrestling on the floor, beer glasses being thrown through the air from one side of the room to the other.

Chapter 6

Seth was fifteen years old now, glad for summer vacation after a year of junior high school. Classes were small at Alton School—caring teachers taught reading, spelling, mathematics, and his favorite subject, history, to mostly eager to learn kids. Summer didn't come soon enough though—he was glad to forego trousers, collared shirt, and shoes, for shorts, a T-shirt, and being barefoot.

During summer vacation, he had more time to go into the dining room while his father was having breakfast or lunch and read to him from one of the books he borrowed from Katie, one that she thought might stimulate Will as well as Seth. Will was often responsive—he'd smile and mention to customers that despite his blond hair, the good-looking curly-black-haired kid with the dark complexion was his—of course many of the older folks remembered Seth's mother and her classic Italian beauty. Seth had become tall and slim like his father—with his classic and rugged good looks, so handsome it was easy to imagine him the wandering movie cowboy, his hat pulled down low as he rode slowly into town to fight the bad guys and win the girl. On the other hand, many times Will was quiet and detached. Seth understood, he was taught to be patient with his father, to spend time talking and reading to him.

On a hot, humid day during the summer of 1959, he was walking down a path that spun-off from Mexico Road, zigzagging through the thick woods, leading to Lorraine Lake. He was searching for some frogs or snakes, and maybe one of those hard-to-find stone arrowheads left behind hundreds of years ago by an Indian hunting party. Mr. Dengler would bring to school many from his personal collection and allow students to examine each one closely. He was told Dengler would again be his history teacher in ninth grade—he was delighted—he'd hear more of the wise old man's exciting stories and interesting tales of adventure that made the young curious student's mind wander, thinking about those savage hunters and how Mexico Road was born as one of their narrow paths, just like the offspring paths that he now hiked trying to find some of his own treasure.

Occasionally Dengler would shock the kids from their daydreams by slapping a shiny silver dollar on his desk and challenging any student who could tell him the important fact from the lesson he just mentioned. If any student could, they got the silver dollar. During all the years he was teaching, no one ever remembers him giving a silver dollar away.

Seth came upon Martha Dern sitting and reading a book in the cool shade under an aged large oak tree along the small ten-acre lake's bank, right where Antietam Creek flows into it. She heard his feet cracking the twigs and dead leaves covering the ground, then screamed and ran for a distance into the pasture as fast as she could, stopping and spinning around, then shouting across the field, "Who are you, and what do you want?" He froze, wishing he could be like some type of wildlife, undetected if totally still. Shocked and stunned, he never expected to meet anyone along the path, certainly not a girl, and never a girl that beautiful. He tried his best to display a cavalier attitude—he hollered a lie, "I noticed you sitting here and I wanted to say hello."

She started to walk toward him barefoot across the open space through the thick grass. She yelled back, "Don't even think about trying any funny stuff." He didn't know what she considered "funny stuff." He decided not to ask.

Still a distance from him, she told him her name, asked what his was, and told him she lived a mile down Mexico Road on her parent's farm. She was also fifteen years old but didn't attend Seth's school—instead a student at the one-room schoolhouse run by the church her family belonged to, a very small ultra-conservative fringe sect of the Brethren Church numbering about three hundred members. They were known, like other Brethren, as "Dunkards," which means to dip. When Dunkards are baptized, always after reaching adulthood, they're dipped into the water three times—face forward as each name of the Trinity is recited. Sect members believe they, as God's chosen people, are the only ones going to heaven.

Like Amish, they're pacifists and don't allow music, theatre, or dancing. Unlike the Amish, they use modern conveniences such as electricity and automobiles. Men wear modern clothing—the women, including the young girls like Martha, dress in home sewn colorful printed dresses of lightweight fabric with a hemline below the knees, closed leather or canvass shoes with laces, and green or blue knee-high wool stockings during the winter.

Cautiously she walked closer to him. Now he got a closer look at her beautiful face with perfect features and glowing blue eyes—she stood five feet tall with a flawlessly proportioned body, had long chestnut brown hair, and like all the women in her church, she had it pulled back and pinned up into a bun under a small and stiff white mesh bonnet worn on the back of her head, a symbol of piety, with two long thin ribbon ties left dangling on each side of her face reaching down to the bust line. She had full eyebrows, a small straight nose, and brimming sensuous lips.

For Seth, meeting her was prophetic, as if she was the one who posed for a small old painting of a young nineteenth-century German maiden that has hung for years on one of the inn's dining room walls. Encased in a drab green 8" x 10" chipped and scratched wood frame, and probably bought at some flea market years earlier, the print showed the young girl wearing a dark, heavy black dress and bonnet of old country Germany. It hung there all during his youth defining for him the beauty of women. With each phase of his maturing he saw her differently—first as his young mother, next a sister or cousin, then a classmate, now a girlfriend, and soon a wife.

It was unsettling for Martha, raised in a very conservative lifestyle, to be in front of a strange boy barefoot and dressed only in her bra and panties. Seth's wish, natural for any boy his age, was to see her without any clothing on at all, but he had been taught to be empathetic. Instead of giggling and pointing a finger in mocking gesture, he picked up her dress lying under the tree and handed it to her. "It's too late now, there isn't too much embarrassment left in me," she remarked curtly—she had a hearty voice for a girl. The anguished look on her face made him feel terrible, he knew he had invaded her privacy, but also in the context of her very conservative upbringing, also violated some of her innocence. He could only apologize. The unexpected meeting shocked her, but within minutes his poise made her feel more comfortable. She was leaving down her guard—she had never done that before—possibly allowing herself to become infatuated with a boy so very unlike the immature ones at her school.

She invited him to sit with her and have a glass of lemonade, brought from home in a large glass jar she kept chilled by submerging it in the creek. They sat next to each other on a rock ledge—she was dangling her bare feet into the cool, rapidly moving water. When he pointed out that she only had one glass, she teasingly asked, "We'll share, you don't have any weirdo germs, do you?" He answered, "No, it's just that we don't share glasses at home."

She was pouring the lemonade from the jar while he was asking her about the paperback book she was reading—a mystery novel about a teenage heroine who was a private detective. "I love mystery and detective stories—especially Sherlock Holmes, but I'm not allowed to read 'em, but I do anyhow. Most of the girls at school sneak into the used bookstore in Rossville and buy 'em." She was talking non-stop as if she never had anybody to share her thoughts and experiences with before. "We hide 'em in the girl's outhouse in back of the school, and then swap 'em during recess or lunch. The elders forbid us reading these types of books, they've ruled they encourage idleness and immorality—we're only allowed to read the Scriptures and schoolbooks." She only stopped long enough to take a sip of lemonade. "One of the boys in school got into big trouble when he gave a report on a magazine story that said Earth is just a speck of dust in the universe." She couldn't help laughing while telling the story. "He had to go to counseling sessions with one of the deacons. That's the kind of school I go to!"

She took another sip of lemonade from the glass. "I especially like to solve the crime before the book tells me all the clues and solutions, I think I'd make a good detective." She refilled the glass, passed it to him, and after taking a sip he spit out a lemon seed. She hollered, "No! Don't spit out the seeds, swallow 'em, they're God's precious work, the beginnings of life, put 'em inside you—have some God!" Seth explained, "I gag eating any kind of seed." She cupped her hands under his mouth, and he spit out half a dozen seeds. She put them in her mouth, swallowed them, and asked, "Are you positively sure you don't have any weirdo germs?" Before he could answer that question again, they both fell back on her blanket, laughing loudly, eyes closed to shield them from the bright blue sunlit sky.

They lay there, telling each other about their families and their very different schools. He decided he'd tell her later his family owned the Oregon Inn. She told him her family speaks mostly German at home—the Pennsylvania Dutch dialect—

in her school only English is spoken—it's the parent's responsibility to teach the dialect to the children. "My father is a farmer, my two older brothers help him, and my mother keeps house and I go to school and work at our produce booth at the market."

She recounted how her walks in the woods take her to this private hideaway for relief from the summer heat, allowing her to take off her dress and go barefoot, and sometimes, but not that day, even removing her bonnet and unpinning her long hair, letting it fall down her back—all improper behavior for a Brethren woman except in the home, and if married, in the presence of her husband. Relieved by the forest's cooler air, she'd take a forbidden book and travel to a faraway place—a Caribbean island, Paris, the great wall in China, Damascus—to find clues to murders and uncover secret plots of espionage. Seth was awestruck by the beauty of every part of her—fixing his eyes on her perfect lips, gleaning each word flowing through them, glimpsing away for an occasional second, careful not to stymie her with his stare. He already knew that she was special—any artist would want to paint her face with the inviting blue eyes, and her velvety, alabaster skin. He wanted to hold her, kiss her—he wanted to be in love with her.

She wanted to know about him, so he talked about his love of history. "I look for Indian arrowheads, there are a lot around here because this area was Indian hunting grounds." He loved being alone while he hunted for wildlife and relics but didn't want to tell her he valued solitude more than most boys his age—he'd have to admit he explored the woods to escape his home life. "What are the chances of you finding an arrowhead here in these large woods?" Pleased that she was interested, he was glad for the opportunity to impress her, to show his knowledge about something—anything. "I only ever found one, and I think I was very lucky to find it, but the Indians did hunt here for hundreds, maybe thousands of years, so I guess there are pretty many lying around if somebody looks hard enough."

She sat up suddenly, as if startled. "I can't believe that I'm actually sitting here in the woods, barefoot, without a dress on, with you!" She had never been allowed to be with a boy without a chaperone, especially with one not a member of her church who could put worldly ideas into her head. Thoughts were racing through her mind to justify the situation—she was here with him because he found her by accident, circumstances she couldn't have avoided. It wasn't her fault that he strolled down that path and walked into her life.

It was getting late in the afternoon. "Do you have any mystery or detective books at home? I'd be interested in borrowing one, if you have any, that is." He never read a mystery or detective book, but he was reasonably sure that his grandmother had some books like that. "If you meet me tomorrow, I'll loan you one or two." He was thrilled when she agreed, his heartbeat rapid as the adrenalin raced through his veins. He was ready to do cartwheels but came to his senses just in time, reminding himself she seemed impressed with his confident and reserved demeanor—he was being so unlike other fifteen-year-old boys.

She showed him a coffee can she kept buried up against the large tree's trunk. She put her mystery paperback book in the can, snapped on the lid, and placed it under some twigs and pieces of sod. They started up the path to Mexico Road— he carried her blanket and the lemonade jar. She was carrying her shoes, tiptoeing and hop scotching to avoid stones gouging the soles of her bare feet, enduring the discomfort, yelling "Ouch!" every few steps. "Do you live near that den of sin, the Oregon Inn?" He lied, telling her he lived on a farm about a mile away. At Mexico Road they parted, she went left—he turned right to go to the inn. He walked a while, then turned around and watched her from a distance slowly dancing along, still tiptoeing, raising her free arm as if balancing on a high wire. She turned around and waved at him, somehow knowing he'd be watching her disappear down the ribbon of white stones.

As he walked he began to fantasize—thoughts seemed to be banging into each other as they swirled inside his head.

Whenever he saw men with their wives on their arm, he was curious how they came together—he noticed the happiest seemed to be the ones who mentioned they fell in love with the special woman they believed was set aside for them by God's plan or some kind of mystical fate. The chance that this could happen to him always felt out of reach—until now.

Unable to sleep, he tossed and turned the whole night, coming to the breakfast table looking disheveled. Katie, always the wise grandmother, asked, "What's bothering you? You look like you haven't slept for a week." Seth wanted to brush aside her questions. "I'm OK, I didn't feel too good during the night." Katie wasn't worried—she knew lovesickness when she saw it. "Does your trouble sleeping have anything to do with that girl that phoned this morning asking for you? She said her name was Martha." Defensive, he jumped from his chair. "Martha? That must be the Brethren girl I saw at the lake yesterday, I said hello to her." Katie started laughing while watching him act like girls weren't of any interest to him. "Seth, it's OK if you meet a girl, as long as you behave yourself, soon you'll be able to go to dances at school, maybe you can ask this Martha to a dance." He was trying to end the conversation, feeling more and more uncomfortable. "I told you she's Brethren, she doesn't go to my school, and she certainly doesn't dance." He started for the door just as Henrietta came into the room—glad to escape before his aunt's teasing made things worse. "I'm not gonna go to any dances anyway, I don't know why she phoned me, I'm going outside." He was carrying one of Katie's many paperback books that she always coaxed him to read, a mystery—it was for Martha. Henrietta asked, "What's his problem?" Katie explained, "He's in love, and it's eating him up from the inside out."

Eventually he became comfortable talking to Katie about Martha. When she went to the market she sought her out and introduced herself. Martha was flattered, surprised that the woman wanted to meet her, and soon Katie's trips to the market started with lunch or a snack with the young girl. They talked and became close—Katie gave her advice when asked, and kept reassuring her that having problems while growing up is normal, and a lot of persistence was needed to pave the road to future happiness. They also talked about Seth.

After taking flight out the kitchen door he went straight to the hideaway to meet her. "I hope I didn't get you in trouble phoning your house, I never phoned a boy before." He was pleased she called, but wished he had answered the phone and kept her a secret. "How did you get my phone number, my family's name isn't in the phone book?" Her keen sense of observation, and a good memory, helped her when she needed information. "I figured you lived at the Oregon Inn all along, did you forget that I'm a detective?" He seemed a little agitated rather than impressed. She explained, "Good detectives never tell how they solve a case, but I'll tell you how I suspected you lived at the Oregon Inn. Your aunt buys potatoes from my family at the market, one day you were standing there with her, you didn't notice me, but I noticed you, especially with all that black curly hair on top of your head. My mother told me your aunt is the manager of the Oregon Inn."

He apologized for not being truthful. "I didn't want you to have a reason for us not to be friends, the Oregon Inn doesn't have a very good reputation." She tried to reassure him. "I wouldn't blame you for things other people, including your family, did." She understood Seth's anxiety—she had her own circumstances of the past that could easily scare a suitor away. "The lady I talked to when I phoned said she was your grandmother, she seems very nice." He assured her that his relatives aren't all murdering gangsters. "She's the best grandmother anybody could ever have—she's my father's mother. My mother was Italian—I got my black hair from her—just like my Aunt Henrietta's. My mother died giving birth to me."

Martha's dream of becoming a detective—an impossible ambition for a Brethren girl growing up in rural Pennsylvania—made her determined to eventually renounce the church's lifestyle. Only Rebecca, her mother, took her resolve seriously, much more sympathetic than most Brethren mothers. Age had only slightly diminished Rebecca's good looks, in many ways improved with maturity. Under her bonnet was beautiful light brown hair with blue eyes set in a pretty face that made obvious the source of her daughter's beauty. She recognized that she had a melancholy daughter who was unusually bright. When Martha asked if she could take walks in the woods instead of helping with the household chores that would prepare her to be a wife and mother, Rebecca consented, keeping it from the men of the family. "Where's Martha?" asked Walter Dern, her strict and serious father, speaking German—most of the Pennsylvania Dutch did—old and young alike, including Martha, when there weren't any outsiders present "The garden needs tending, she needs to get her work done!" His stern words were reminders that the women of Brethren farming households are responsible for the family vegetable garden. Walter was a man of the earth—his hands were calloused, his body trim and firm from the hard labor that was part of his everyday life. He had a full head of coarse brown hair—there were deep lines on his always-tanned, clean shaven face, and he had large dark brown eyes. His two sons, both older than Martha, worked on the farm with him. Serious confrontation with her was avoided mostly because Walter was much too busy to pay a great deal of attention to the excuses Rebecca made for her, or to follow up on them. Rebecca coped with the anxiety, knowing the life her fifteen-year-old daughter was expected to live wasn't going to satisfy her.

Seth and Martha began meeting every couple of days—by midsummer every afternoon—at the lakeside hideaway. They lay in the tall thick grass, talked, played games, read, giggled, and sometimes chased each other across the pasture. They were becoming comfortable being with each other, but had the typical apprehensions of the young, questioning whether the other would accept them despite the complications in their lives. They were beginning to sense the adversity they lived with was the reason they were being drawn together.

Katie had often told him to use the atmosphere he was growing up in, witnessing all the sinning and the misery it causes, to learn life's lessons. "Your experiences now will help you develop character, use good judgment, and become a better person. Never forget that a price must always be paid for immorality."

He wanted Martha to understand the reality of his situation. While most boys his age might witness men drink, smoke, curse, and eat too much, he was exposed to cases of stolen and untaxed whiskey and other contraband, the transporting and sale of heroin, cocaine, and marijuana, he was witnessing prostitution, lewdness by many inn patrons, illegal gambling, horse-race fixing, acts of violence, and all kinds of other dreadful behavior. Katie, as usual, was right—living every day surrounded by all that sinning caused him to develop an early sophistication and worldly awareness of life, plus a very necessary surplus of self-confidence. It was this self-confidence, more than anything else that attracted Martha to him. She needed a friend—she had been hostile toward her father, her brothers, her relatives, the church elders, her schoolteachers, and her classmates—refusing to accept a future as a Brethren farmer's wife. She wanted Seth for a friend because he had patience, and understood her wanting to live her life the way she pleased. He thought eventually he could control her—in a good way— if only to keep her from harming herself. Maybe he'd become the only person who could control her—if that came to pass, it'd be because she loved him—he wanted that because he'd have the opportunity to love her back.

She had one or two girlfriends, mostly insecure and unattractive girls nobody else wanted as a friend. Boys were always flirting with her—wanting to court her, despite her efforts to make them dislike her. Each time she rejected a boy, or chose not to attend church socials or school functions, more pressure was put upon her.

Until her fifteenth birthday in April 1959, and before she and Seth met, Martha had done a lot of babysitting—the job served more than one purpose. It gave her the chance to earn extra money for her family, and her parent's couldn't pressure her to attend social affairs—mostly held at the same time she was working. She was highly recommended—young Brethren girls are more trusted because they're taught at a young age to care for the children of friends and family members, getting prepared for motherhood.

She was tending Fred and Janet Holt's three-year-old daughter Mary almost every weekend at some time or the other. The Holts, in there mid-thirties and wealthy, were able to live in a large beautiful home on top of the hill overlooking Alton Manor because Janet inherited her father's large hardware store in Rossville. Fred was a balding but tall and handsome man who wore black-framed glasses, expensive suits for work, and the best sport coats and sweaters for social occasions. Janet was overweight but attractive. She dyed her hair orange red and wore it teased into a large bouffant style, and wore expensive bright-colored dresses, long gaudy earrings, spiked high-heel shoes, and a lot of makeup.

Janet treated Martha like a domestic servant, but Fred was always kind to her—he was the one who paid her and then drove her home. One afternoon he stopped by the produce booth to pay her when Walter and Rebecca were away. While Martha was helping customers he picked up a large green apple, the tart kind used mostly for baking, and bit into it with delight as he felt the saliva glands in his mouth react with furious quivering. He began some small talk. "How's school going?" She nodded in bored reaction to the question she had been asked so many times before, especially by the customers and friends of her parents who had watched her grow from a little girl to a young woman. He asked her if she had a boyfriend. "I don't have time for boys, the boys I go to school with act like two-year-olds." He laughed. "If you ever wanna be with a man, you let me know, and I'm serious."

He was making her feel uncomfortable, but she wasn't convinced he was serious until she saw a look of desire on his face, an awful, lustful grin she had never seen on a man before, but no young girl could mistake it for what it was. She looked down on the ground to break eye contact, feeling embarrassed, wanting to believe he momentarily lost his senses, hoping he'd leave so she wouldn't have to feel so uneasy.

A few days later while driving her home late at night, he pulled off the road and stopped the car. "Martha, I know you're only fifteen years old, and I want to apologize for what I said to you at the market." She felt relieved, then lied. "That's OK, Mr. Holt, I didn't give it any more thought." Her relief was short-lived. "Well that disappoints me, I thought you'd at least consider having sex with me. You young girls all wanna act so innocent, but I know most of you aren't." Looking over at her, he sighed and turned his head, staring out the windshield. "You're so beautiful, you're driving me nuts. I thought teenage girls were always horny." She was getting scared. "You don't have to bullshit me, I know you want it. That Hartman kid that everyone knows you're screwing isn't old enough to appreciate a girl like you." He leaned over and put his large hand around the back of her head and pulled her head toward him. He went to kiss her but she resisted, pulling away from him. Crying now, she yelled out, "Please, just take me home!" She raised her left arm, and used her hand to push him away. When he resisted she scratched his face, her fingernails making deep tracks into his skin. He cried out, slapping his hand on his cheek to check the blood seeping from her marks. Seeing the rage on his face and deciding not to wait for him to recover, she opened the car door and ran into the woods, staying there about ten minutes until he finally made a U-turn, heading back to his house. She walked home in tears.

She had been prepared to fight him with all her strength, but had decided, when she was younger, if she ever found herself in this type of situation, getting away and letting it pass was the best way of handling it. She believed that these types of men might very well offer no resistance to her violent retaliation, or then again they might panic, become enraged and harm her.

Mr. Geer, her handsome twenty-two year old piano teacher, had sat next to her on the bench when she was thirteen years old and put his hand on her thigh, making her feel very uncomfortable. A few weeks later he asked her if she'd be willing to sit on his lap. She began laughing uncontrollably, and he got very angry. He stopped giving her lessons, sending his associate, Miss Dotsy, instead, explaining to her that Martha was developing a crush on him.

When she was fourteen years old deacon Marvin Fick asked her to stay after youth meeting and help him set up tables and chairs for Bible class. After the work was done he held her head between his two hands, and as she tried to pull away, he forced a kiss on her lips just as his wife walked in. The deacon hurried from the room as Mary Fick stood there in stunned silence. When she regained her composure she took Martha aside and warned her that she'd tell her parents if she ever again tempted her husband to commit adultery!

Janet Holt came to the market to confront Walter and Rebecca, staring at Martha while ranting. "You keep your little slut daughter away from my husband, do you understand? I heard about her reputation!" Her nostrils flaring, she displayed rage Martha never imagined would ever be directed at her. Walter asked, "What are you talking about? And please don't call my daughter such a terrible name." Rebecca interjected, "Mrs. Holt, tell us what has you so upset." Calming down, she growled, "Ask your daughter, she seems to think it's all right to proposition a thirty-four year old married man." Walter and Rebecca, both shocked, turned to Martha, who was standing there motionless. Janet Holt continued her tirade. "Last night while Fred was driving her home she asked him if he wanted to park in the woods, she wanted to have sex with him! When he refused, she became enraged and reached over and scratched his face. He almost lost control of the car!" Walter, staying calm, said, "I'll talk to my daughter, I appreciate you coming to us. I'm sorry you're upset. She'll be apologizing to you and your husband."

Janet Holt told everyone she knew, and began telling anybody else who'd listen, that fifteen-year-old Martha Dern had tried to seduce her husband.

Walter told Martha to walk home—he'd talk to her later that night after the market closed. After she left, Rebecca expressed doubts. "I think Fred Holt got after her, and she reacted the way I'd want her to. I'm proud of her and I'm gonna tell her that." Walter scolded her—he had always known Rebecca coddled the girl entirely too much. "Even if what you say is true, it's only because she encouraged him. She thinks she's too good for boys, now she wants to tease married men. She needs to be punished."

The Dern house was a white slate-shingled two-story house with a large screened porch used for sleeping during hot, humid summer nights. The typical farm smells—from the manure or chicken house—rarely permeated into the house. Instead there were always wonderful, lingering smells of good food as a result of Rebecca cooking soups, baking pies and cakes, or roasting meat. The house was filled with modest furniture, much of it passed down from previous generations— but not antique.

That night when Walter wanted to confront Martha, she refused to unlock her bedroom door—he was forced to do his shouting from the hallway. "You're gonna go see the bishop and tell him what you did and ask him to lead you in prayer—

confessing your sins and asking the Lord for mercy and forgiveness." He felt hurt. Suspecting his daughter wanted to become sexually active was difficult enough for this rigid and reverent man, but he was devastated when told she was willing to commit adultery. "You're gonna write Mr. and Mrs. Holt and ask for their forgiveness, and you're gonna promise your mother that you will live a life of virtue, a young woman who will go to her marriage bed a virgin!"

The next day Rebecca wrote to Fred and Janet Holt: "I'm sorry if I caused any problems between both of you. Please forgive me. I promise it will never happen again." She signed Martha's name, and mailed it.

The church elders were now questioning whether she had a healthy attitude about Christian marriage. They advised Walter and Rebecca to be firm with their "difficult" daughter and keep her associations within the church, avoiding unwholesome influences from people that lived lives that contradict the spoken word.

That spring, just a month before she met Seth, Walter ordered her to accompany a young boy to a church youth picnic. He became impatient when she resisted, shouting, "Is there something wrong with you girl, don't you know that God intends you to mate with a man!" Rebecca watched the confrontation for a while, then to encourage family peace, chose to plead with her. "Martha, just go to this picnic, that's all we want you to do—do this one thing for your father. He wants to be proud of you." She fell to the floor screaming, "Never!" holding her hands over her ears, crying and kicking her feet. Walter looked down at her then flashed a cold glance at Rebecca before leaving the room. Martha, keeping her ears covered, got up and ran to her bed. Rebecca realized by this time her daughter wasn't going to marry a Brethren farmer and spend her life as a farm wife giving birth every year or two.

Martha wanted a career, have a husband only if he encourages her, treats her as an equal, and shares the responsibilities of raising their children. She realized she had to prepare to meet those very challenges because she and Seth were falling in love.

Seth always dreaded the end of summer, losing the freedom a young boy has growing up in the country paradise that Mexico Road passes through. Now, to make matters worse, he had a girlfriend that he wouldn't be seeing as much because she'd be going back to her school, working at the market, and going to church services and activities that he wasn't welcome at. He couldn't phone her—she told him her parents would want to know all the details if a boy called her. "I'll be in big trouble if my father or brothers ever find out that you and I are meeting," she warned.

Fall arrived on cue, preparing everyone for the cold and harshness of winter. He got to see her occasionally at the market, offering to go with Henrietta to help carry the bags of groceries to the car. Sometimes they had the chance to talk while Rebecca and Henrietta chatted—he'd use some of the few minutes they had to slip her another one of Katie's mystery paperbacks. She noticed that he was growing taller while she wasn't—she was still five feet tall. He said, "Evidently God's finished with you, he knows he got you just right—but with me he's still trying to grow me from a goofy kid to a grown up guy." Martha laughed, looked around to see if there were eavesdroppers, and then whispered, "I think you're pretty good-looking, and just remember my opinion is all that matters."

Christmas was a difficult time for them. They were expected to show feelings of joy while prevented from being together on Christmas Eve and Christmas day. They felt isolated and alone—Martha was forced to be with family and friends who didn't know about him, if they did they wouldn't allow it. For Seth, he had to deal with Aunt Henrietta, who was not pleased that he had a Brethren girlfriend, and his father and grandmother, not yet ready to take any romance involving him seriously, and insensitive to his moping because they had forgotten or never knew the gut wrenching feelings that lovesickness brings on.

On the day after Christmas the market opened early morning for business as usual, all the merchants were rushed, the aisles were crowded with shoppers, the Derns always did a brisk produce business that day. Martha met Seth at the lunch counter as soon as she could get her first break.

Chapter 7

Seth turned sixteen years old in March 1960. Katie and Henrietta had decided to have a birthday party for him but changed their minds when he reminded them that most of the parents of his classmates wouldn't allow their kids to come to the Oregon Inn. Certainly Martha wouldn't be allowed to attend, and he couldn't possibly have a very happy birthday party without her being there.

They decided instead to take Seth and Will on a picnic, a good idea because father and son needed time together. They worried that Will wouldn't cooperate, but he did—he only took the pills prescribed by his doctors that day—he laid off the "feel good" drugs that Ganttrano kept feeding him. When the day came he was clear minded and jovial, and truly enjoyed spending the afternoon and evening with his family. It was warmer than expected. Instead of a cold March wind, an early spring breeze was stirring the air.

He teased his son. "Well, do you want to throw some football or run a race? I'm gonna beat your ass doing either!" Seth yowled, "No way, Pop, let's race, let's see how totally out of shape you are!" They ran across the field as fast as they could, side by side, their legs barely keeping up with their feet, and soon Will veered over and tackled his son, bringing him to the ground. They rolled around in the grass, hugging and laughing loudly as the women cheered and applauded. It was a wonderful scene. They ate heartily, and all four finished the day sitting on the inn's second-floor porch, Katie talking about the inn's past, Henrietta about growing up with Magdalena, and then they all quietly listened to the night.

Henrietta, happy seeing how good Will felt and acted that day, knew that the doctor-ordered medication was strong enough to let Sal run his schemes without Will's resistance. Ganttrano, who didn't trust the clinic's pills and feared the possibility of changed or eliminated prescriptions, gave Will pills that put him into a state of near-total incoherence—a cruel overkill. Henrietta knew she couldn't protest. She had to cooperate.

She and Katie realized the predicament they were all in, and the possible consequences—they didn't talk about it. Instinct had taken over, the specifics would remain unspoken.

Martha's sixteenth birthday came on April 4. Seth came to the market with a birthday card, supplied by Katie, and he bought her a cupcake at one of the bakery booths.

She read what he wrote on the card—"Happy birthday, Martha, thank you for coming into my life. Seth." Becoming sixteen, and his birthday card message, gave her that awful young love feeling that scares you because you fear losing it as quickly as you found it. Her feelings for him were growing but so was the fear of being hurt. Allowing her anxiety to show through, she asked, "Oh, Seth, what are we gonna do?"

Later that day he met one of Martha's friends, Naomi, she came to the market to wish her best friend a happy birthday. She was a small, delicate, and timid girl with thin light brown hair tucked under her bonnet, the ribbon ties hanging alongside her small pale, plain face.

According to Naomi, Martha told all the kids in school that Seth was her boyfriend, a relationship she was strictly forbidden to have, and how handsome he was, shocking her schoolmates when she bragged that his family owned the Oregon Inn, the barroom and gambling den that employed prostitutes.

Naomi believed Seth was good for Martha. "She needs you for a lot of reasons, but especially because you take her hopes and dreams seriously, believe they're possible, and want to share 'em with her, and she knows that you'll protect her and keep her safe. I hope you realize you're the only person who really has any influence over her." She was making her case for her friend. Martha had already figured out that Seth someday could spring her from her oppressive lifestyle. "She's a very stubborn and strong willed girl, she gets into trouble in school and at church because she speaks her mind and doesn't let anybody control her, not her parents, the teachers, the church elders—nobody. They all try to stifle her."

She found it titillating that he got to live among all the sin and wasn't held accountable for any of it. He'd tell her about things there, whetting her appetite to hear more. "The prostitutes aren't allowed to take a guy into a room if all he's buying is oral sex—she does him right out in the hall. If someone walks by— those are the breaks," Martha's jaw dropped. "Aren't they embarrassed when people walk by?" He explained that most people who patronize the Oregon Inn engage in behavior they wouldn't be a party to anywhere else. "Prostitutes don't get embarrassed, and the guy's usually too drunk to notice the audience, who are usually other drunks." She began laughing. "How many times do you walk up and down the hall to see the action?" He tried his best to be serious. "As many times necessary to keep furthering my education!"

Now that it was summer they were meeting and spending most weekdays at the Lorraine Lake hideaway, Seth hung around the market on Fridays and Saturdays while she worked at the Dern booth. When she got breaks from working, they sat and talked in the wooded area on the edge of the market's crowded courtyard, holding hands underneath the picnic table. She wanted them to have the same dreams. "I want a career, but I also wanna have children—three boys and three girls!" It was a little scary thinking about being a father to six kids—but if she wanted six kids, then he'd be a father to six kids! He asked, "I remember on the day we met you told me not to try any 'funny stuff.' I never asked you what that meant, but I hope you don't consider me kissing you funny stuff, because I'm gonna kiss you right now." She smiled and closed her eyes. He looked around quickly for any onlookers—he put his lips against hers. The two of them stealing a kiss at the market was dangerous—a young sect member like Martha kissing in public would cause her parents great embarrassment, and if the elders found out about it, the bishop could order her shunned.

No one in her family suspected she was meeting Seth at Lorraine Lake, but Rebecca had noticed her talking to him regularly. She warned, "Don't you get smitten over that boy, he's not one of us, do you understand?" Martha wanted to tell her she'd decide for herself who to have as a boyfriend, not her family or church. Instead, she just nodded, hoping that would satisfy her mother for now, preventing a discussion about it with her father—he'd impose strict restrictions, and enforce them, if he suspected she was starry-eyed over Seth Hartman.

It was a hot and humid day when he kissed her again, this time while they swam in the lake, then he took off his swimming trunks and heaved them ashore while she opened her mouth to mimic shock and surprise. He asked her to take off her clothing. "You shouldn't worry about me seeing you nude, I'm your boyfriend!" She didn't need much encouragement, she took off her bra and threw it ashore, then reached down and removed her panties, holding them up in the air and then tossing them. Then she did what was, to her, probably more significant. She took off her bonnet and unpinned her hair, leaving it fall down her back, the ends touching the water.

He waded over and pressed against her, moving his hands up and down her back and buttocks. They embraced—she put her arms around his neck, tilted her head and parted her lips, he put his tongue in her mouth. They laid under the big tree between two blankets, using their tongues to French kiss, he savored the taste and smell of her while touching and kissing her everywhere, covering her face with his kisses.

Soon he began sneaking downstairs late at night, after the barroom closed, stealing open packs of cigarettes forgotten by customers, and cans of beer from the cooler. At first they coughed as they smoked, and they drank the beer until dizzy. He'd steal whiskey, mixing some with a can of cola, and some they drank straight, setting their throats afire while getting drunk.

Chapter 8

Seth told Martha, soon after they had met, that he would never accept it if his family lost the Oregon Inn. Now that he was getting older, thinking that he and Martha might stay together, he began sharing with her his plans for the future. At first he thought that was a crazy notion, but he had heard men and women tell of marrying their high school sweetheart. Besides, Martha told him she loved him, and he loved her, what else could matter?

He knew there was a very real possibility the inn could slip out of his family's control. Katie was getting older, and because of his father's depression and his mother's death at such a young age, there was a time gap in the order of succession—no family member was young enough or old enough, or healthy enough, to assume management of the inn. He could only hope that he'd be ready soon enough. For now he was powerless to change its unfolding fate, he had to sit tight and hope for the best. Later he could do whatever was necessary to take control and keep the inn in the family.

Later that summer of 1960, Martha got to know Hannah Kaiser, still working as a sales clerk at Jonas's market booth. Hannah took a quick liking to the young girl.

Seth, always coping with his father's suffering, became disturbed when he saw Jonas selling Nazi war souvenirs and relics. Martha was afraid of Jonas—seeing him fly into rages, screaming obscenities in both English and German to people who doubted his appraisals, they'd walk away shaking their heads.

He had become a tall husky man, 6' 4", but still had the pointed nose, thin and oily blond hair, and receding hairline, and now bad teeth, yellowed mostly from chain-smoking obscure, unfiltered European and Turkish brand cigarettes.

He usually called out to Seth when he saw him walking by with Martha. "Hey, aren't you Will Hartman's kid?" He knew the answer, just taunting the boy. "That Italian woman you come here with, is that your aunt?" Seth would just nod yes, look away, and walk by quickly. He kept shouting as he got farther away—"I know your old man—I went to school with him."

Like everybody Martha met—she was always playing detective—Hannah was soon subjected to her questioning. She learned that Hannah was not Jonas's girlfriend—she was Ben Kaiser's wife—one of Jonas's despicable associates.

She told Martha that people were always traveling to the Konrad farm, staying for various lengths of time. Martha was curious why Jonas had all of these friends—"He's such a nasty man." Hannah laughed. "Because we're all Nazis, that's why!" Martha was startled, finding it hard to believe that anyone would admit being a Nazi. She quickly recovered. "I learned about Nazis in school, they killed millions of people and tried to rule the world." Hannah raised her voice. "So many lies! We're dedicated people who meet and talk about how wonderful things will be when the Nazi party rebounds in America!"

Jonas returned and noticed Hannah and Martha talking. He had watched her while she worked at her family's produce booth and daydreamed, like so many other men who worked at the market, about having such a young and beautiful girl.

Men would stop by the Dern's produce booth to chat with her, admiring her slim shape, ample bosom, and pretty face with the blue eyes—flirting with her—it was always going on. She had learned when she was a very young girl, with no help from anyone, to guess men's motives early, overlook their improper advances, smile and attempt to guide the course of conversation, and try not to offend or embarrass them, especially the older men who appreciated her as a woman in a less lustful way, and many times innocently as a daughter.

Jonas's attraction to her was more complicated. He was appreciative of her German ancestry, certainly her blue eyes, her perfect features, a truly beautiful young woman he fancied to be the mother of his perfect Aryan children. When he thought of her being with Will Hartman's half-Italian son, he was repulsed. He warned himself that he could easily become obsessed with the girl, and be unable to accept the reality that she'd never go with him. Obsession would be a menacing diversion, taking time away from his organization and its' mission.

With Martha sitting there, he questioned Hannah. "What are you telling her? She's a troublemaker, she hangs around with Will Hartman's kid." Hannah, looking at Martha admiringly, told him, "She's such a pretty girl, and she's perhaps interested in our cause." Jonas said, "Hah, you gotta be kidding, she's Brethren, they think they're the only people going to heaven." Martha gave him a piercing stare as she stood up to leave, telling Hannah she'd talk to her later.

She was surprised Hannah told her so much—now she wanted to find out more about what went on at the Konrad farm. Over the next few weeks she stopped by the gun booth to see her every chance she got, watching when she was alone while Jonas left to do errands. She took advantage of Hannah, lonely, away from her family in New Jersey and working a boring job, welcoming the chance to chitchat with her. She was telling her things she shouldn't have been. Always the novice detective, Martha sought to exploit the woman's naiveté. She wished she'd attempt to recruit her, but it never happened, suspecting Hannah wasn't allowed to invite anybody to the Konrad farm.

Hannah remarked, "You're lucky to have such a handsome boyfriend." Martha was uncomfortable with that kind of talk. She said, "Hannah, my parents and my brothers don't know that Seth is my boyfriend, if they find out, my father will forbid me to be anywhere near him. Please be careful who's around when you refer to him as my boyfriend." Hannah could appreciate the complications forbidden love brings—she had that experience in her youth. "OK, I understand, but sooner or later they're gonna find out." Martha nodded in agreement—she dreaded the thought of it happening too early. "Later is better at this point."

Standing near a side door of the main market building with Naomi, Martha watched Ben Kaiser drive into the parking lot bringing Hannah to work. A sneering smile was always on his big round face, complementing his arrogance and sarcasm. When Hannah got out of his truck and started walking into the market, Ben began to drive away but stopped the truck when he noticed Hannah waving to her. "So you're the gorgeous little thing Hannah told me about?" She smiled and started to walk away. "Are you a snob like most of you young white capped girls?" Ignoring him, she kept walking, but he kept his truck slowly moving alongside them. He stopped the truck when she got close to the building door and shouted just as she was to step into the market. "Let me know when you're ready to get laid, and I'll show you how good an older man can be." Martha turned around and started walking back to the truck. Naomi, very familiar with her friend's temper, screamed, "Martha, forget him, let's go!" Ignoring her pleas, she walked up to him—he was still looking out the truck door window with his trademark smirk. She said, "If you really want to have some of me, I'll give you a little bit." She spit in his face—paused, spit again, then turned and slowly walked away. Naomi ran as fast as she could. Ben calmly wiped his face with his handkerchief.

Normally the experience would have caused him to fly into a rage, race away in his truck, hitting anything or anybody in his path, and then plot to harass and stalk her. However, he was forced to stay low key because he was on probation for disorderly conduct back in New Jersey, he was driving with a suspended driver's license because he pushed an elderly woman driver through an intersection with his truck because she didn't pull out fast enough after the traffic light turned green. She lost control of her car as he pushed her along, running up onto the sidewalk. He got out of his truck, opened her car door and threatened to kill her if he ever saw her on the road. Two men grabbed him and held him until police arrived. The poor woman had a heart attack and almost died.

He enjoyed confrontation, had a long reputation of fomenting it. Years earlier he had done some plumbing work and overcharged a landlord who refused to pay him until he adjusted the bill. Ben refused and began to harass the tenants for years even though they weren't responsible for the charges.

Later that day when Seth came to the market, Naomi was frantic. "I think this guy might try to hurt her." Seth had no idea who Ben Kaiser was—so he couldn't reassure Naomi or himself that Martha wasn't in danger. He asked, "Where's she at now? I'll talk to her." Naomi, still shaking, said, "Thank you Seth, you're the only person she listens to. If I say anything more to her, she'll never talk to me again."

He found her standing with the crowd in the market's courtyard laughing, clapping, and dancing around to worldly music she was forbidden by her parents and church leaders to listen to. The local band, made up a tall and handsome guy named Ash, he played one of those big upright bass guitars, Ray, the skinny fiddler, and Bob, the chubby rhythm guitar player, played country music—during the 1960s it still had its old-fashioned mountain influence, the precursor to the blue grass specialty, in addition to its continuing obsession with cowboy garb. The band leader, a happy-go-lucky musician named Dallas made his steel guitar twang to the love ballads, the lyrics sung out by his wife Dolly, who wore a white cowboy hat atop her flowing dark brown hair, its dangling draw string pulled up under the chin of her pretty face with its broad smile. The music, about love lost, love won, about good times and bad times, about happiness and sadness, caused Martha's emotions to swirl and swell inside her head.

She loved all kinds of music, listening to it on the radio whenever she could sneak an opportunity. Seth took her hand and led her to the parking lot where they wouldn't be noticed. "Naomi told me what you did, I don't want you to antagonize any of those Nazis, they're dangerous, unpredictable, and can be violent." She didn't balk—keeping silent. He squeezed her hand for emphasis, and gently kissed her on the lips. Acting as her protector exhilarated his manhood—he had her under control for now, unfortunately not for long.

A couple of weeks later, while again walking through the parking lot with Naomi, Martha spotted Ben's truck and noticed his wallet lying on the front seat. She stepped up on the running board and emptied it of all the cash—$200, and threw it back on the seat. Naomi was shocked by Martha's brazen act. "You're crazy, they're gonna lock you up someday." Martha strutted along counting the cash. "Naomi, just keep your mouth shut, and don't call me crazy." She walked up to a man walking with his wife and four kids, all unwashed, wearing dirty, tattered clothing—they were obviously very poor, he was carrying a worn canvas shopping bag with some potatoes and vegetables they had just bought. Martha talked quickly. "Sir, I just won this money in a drawing, I'm Brethren, I'm not allowed to keep it. Would you please take it so my parents don't find out I was gambling?" Before the man could say anything, she put the money in his hand. Naomi, looking back as they hurried away, yelled to the surprised family, "Don't tell anybody or we'll get in trouble, just spend the money, buy some more food or something!"

Later in the day Martha saw Ben sitting with Hannah, and she went over to him. "I wanna compliment you for your donation. Giving $200 to help disadvantaged people is a wonderful gesture—thank you!" He instinctively reached for his wallet—he realized it wasn't in his pant's pocket. He jumped up, knocking his chair over, and ran outside to his truck. He found the wallet, its contents strewn all over the seat and floor, all his cash missing! He screamed, "That little thieving goddamn bitch!" He couldn't retaliate, that was frustrating to him, because of his problems back in New Jersey, and he was afraid she'd tell Hannah about him propositioning her.

She was standing sideways, leaning back against the doorframe with her hands behind her back, teasing him by sucking on a lollipop. She smiled as he calmly walked through the doorway, neither saying a word. In the past he had made many tough men scared—they drew back when he walked past them, but this sixteen-year-old girl wasn't afraid of him. She didn't even flinch—he wondered if she feared anything.

A few weeks later, Jonas returned from doing errands in a bad mood while Martha and Hannah were laughing over some silly talk. He gave her a fierce look. "Get your skinny ass away from my booth, I don't want you hanging around here. You're a troublemaker and a goddamn crook. Go find your 'wop' boyfriend and let him entertain you."

That night Naomi phoned Seth and told him about Martha's latest confrontation with Jonas. The next day at the lake he confronted her. "I told you to stay away from those guys, they're capable of doing anything." She was now defying him. "I need to find out what they're up to, I think there's something really bad going on at his farm." Seth responded, "No kidding, that's why I don't want you hanging around with any of 'em." She tried to make him understand that her friendship with Hannah would enable her to find out information. "She's a very nice woman, she's fun to talk to, she likes animals, flowers. She asked me all about my family, my church, and about you." He was getting angry. "She told you she's a Nazi, she stays at the Konrad farm with her husband and other crazy bastards, a farm owned by some nut who's family has wanted to harm mine for years, and what the hell do you do, you talk to her about me and my family!" Martha spoke up. "I didn't tell her about you or your family, I don't know anything about your family. I just mentioned you to her." He cut her off. "Stay away from her, she's just trying to get information about my father and the inn so she can tell Jonas."

Her curiosity and dreams of becoming a detective prompted her to climb out her first-floor bedroom window a few nights later at about 2 AM, walk two miles south on Mexico Road and then down the dark Konrad lane to the big stone farmhouse. It was a warm, still night, with a bright moon providing her with some light, but less cover—she had to be very cautious. It only now occurred to her that the big and vicious watchdogs would surely bark as she got closer. She sat under a tree trying to figure out how to solve that problem when a pickup truck came in the lane. The dogs went berserk, jumping and yanking at their leashes, barking at the approaching truck, and she broke toward the lighted springhouse window, climbing up and standing on an old metal barrel to peer in.

She saw Jonas and Rudolf placing a cadaver into the oven. Horrified, she quickly got scared that she could be harmed, she jumped off the barrel, knocking it over, and ran as fast as she could, falling down several times, suffering scrapes on her knees and elbows. The dogs heard the barrel fall over and started acting up and barking again, this time tipping off the men inside that something unusual was happening outside. She reached the end of the Konrad lane in a state of panic, gasping for air, her heart beating so fast it felt like it was going to explode.

She started walking north on Mexico Road, pausing every few steps, still trying to catch her breath. Fear returned, much stronger, now it was terror and panic, when she saw the same pickup truck that had earlier come down the lane now racing out the lane, swerving, kicking up dust, the driver using his deer-spotting searchlight in search of the intruder. Martha ran off the road and fell into the high grass, hoping that she'd miss the bright probing light beam as it moved about rapidly in its search. She now recognized the pickup truck—it was Ben Kaiser's, and Ben was the driver. Stopping at the end of the lane, he shined the spotlight down Mexico Road, first to the south and then to the north, the truck now standing still, engine idling while he was deciding what to do next. She was lying so close she could feel the hot exhaust blowing over her body— desperately trying not to choke from the fumes, knowing her coughs would give her away. After a few minutes he raced back down the lane zigzagging in reverse gear, slamming the truck door and reentering the house. She stood up and ran as fast as her legs could carry her, falling down some more, one time losing one of her shoes. She didn't take time to find it in the dark—she kept running the best she could, limping with one shoeless foot treading into the stones. She climbed back through the open window into her bed, sweaty, shaking, and sobbing. Finally regaining her breath, somehow she dozed off. She awakened in the morning from a brief troubled sleep, fear returned to her the second she opened her eyes. Rebecca had failed trying to wake her, so she went to the market without her.

Martha had imagined herself to be a better detective then she turned out to be. All the mistakes she made the terrifying night before convinced her she'd have to do better next time. Allowing herself to become surprised and shocked caused her to fall off the barrel, causing the dogs to bark loudly, alerting the Nazis someone was watching them. She knew they wouldn't give up until they found out who was sneaking around that night.

Seth was waiting for her at the market. They usually met at the hideaway on non-market days, but he wanted to swim in the lake on this hot and humid day. After she asked Rebecca for the day off, he started out. They couldn't leave at the same time—it would rouse suspicion they were meeting. She was surprised and glad Seth didn't notice her haggard and troubled appearance—she was still shaken from the night before. Hannah noticed her and called out, "How's the pretty girl doing today?" Martha walked over to her, plopped down, and with a sigh and weak smile, replied, "I really don't feel very well."

Jonas returned from doing his banking, yelling at some kids playing at one of the entrances. "You goddamn brats better find some other place to play. Go outside—get the hell out of here!" After ending that tirade, he noticed Martha sitting with Hannah. "I told you to stay away from my booth, you're a fuckin crook!" Tired and frazzled, in no mood to be confronted, she jumped up and grabbed a heavy plaster paperweight shaped into the form of a swastika from the merchandise table and threw it at him, shouting wildly, "Kiss my ass!" The paperweight hit him on the forehead and he staggered back, putting both hands over the wound—he was dizzy, shocked by the unexpected attack. "You bitch, I'll have you arrested!" Hannah leapt to her feet and went to help him regain his balance, then told her, "You better go over to your family."

An hour later a police officer showed up at the Dern produce booth to question her. "I thought he was gonna hit me, he's a mean man." The police officer told a visibly shaken Walter and Rebecca that perhaps he could convince Jonas not to press charges. "If I'm successful in doing that, I'd suggest the girl gets some counseling. I've talked to some people around here, they tell me that she can be very explosive—there's been problems before." He brought up the stolen-money incident. "There seems to be an issue of theft that should've been reported when it happened, I'm not going to investigate that if we can get everyone happy." Walter, hearing the latest about his errant daughter, decided she should go live with her elderly grandmother and aunt in the mountain town of Orbachville, home to a few hundred people about eighty miles away. It was a village consisting of a small country store, a filling station, small wooden houses and one of the sect's larger schools and churches. He was confident she'd flourish in this more conservative church community, begin living a life of piety, finish school, learn to keep house, get married and bear children.

Jonas said he wouldn't press charges, "As long as they keep the crazy bitch away from me!"

A church elder drove her to Orbachville the next day— she never had a chance to say goodbye to Seth. He had waited at the hideaway the day before, he knew something happened. In the morning Naomi phoned him and told him they took her away, and why they did it. He went to her house but stopped short of knocking on the door knowing that his showing up there would only make her life more difficult. Eighty-five miles is equal to the other side of the world when you're a sixteen-year-old kid living in 1960s rural Pennsylvania. He was already imagining her falling in love with a Brethren boy, getting married, and having her six kids with him. He waited for over a month before he got his first letter from her, written and mailed in secret. She wrote, "Seth, maybe you'll fall in love with someone new, but you'll never find anyone who loves you more than I do." She promised she'd write often.

Bitter, and convinced he lost her, he resolved to get her out of his mind as quickly and as completely as possible to limit the hurt he knew he'd be feeling. Heartbroken, he never answered her letter.

Chapter 9

When Bill Ganttrano had moved into the Oregon Inn eleven years earlier, it didn't take him long to discover Jonas Konrad's gun and war souvenir booth at the market. He was attracted to guns because his personality had that twist that associated guns with power over people—judging them and carrying out punishment. His wartime service gave him an ever-increasing appetite for violence—he missed being in combat when he had new opportunities everyday to kill people.

He had smuggled home from Germany some stolen war artifacts, and Jonas bought them for a fair price. When he offered to sell Jonas marijuana, cocaine, heroin, and pills of any variety, they became fast friends, or at least the closest either of them ever came to having a friend. Jonas recognized that doing business with Ganttrano had at least three advantages. First, it'd now be easy to supply his soldiers with drugs, a terrific incentive to keep them working hard for no pay except room and board. Secondly, he could insist he order Eva Harrison to give him preferential treatment when he patronized the prostitutes. The third advantage was having an excellent source for information about his archenemy Will Hartman.

After a few months, Jonas started to introduce Bill to the soldiers. Because he was Italian, he wasn't allowed to become part of the inner circle, but they all found it easy to treat a drug dealer warmly. Soon after, at Ganttrano's urging, Jonas ordered Ben and Rudolf to send soldiers into Rossville's back alleys to sell drugs, providing even bigger profits for him and for Jonas's Nazi activities.

Like his father, Jonas always had to struggle financially to support the effort, but now drug dealing was bringing in money, making it easier to recruit soldiers—many of them junkies— being able to offer them drugs, whiskey, and beer if they stayed on. They were mostly petty thieves, wife and girlfriend beaters, child molesters—some of them violent social misfits obsessed with guns, knives, and in some cases explosives. They relished getting high on everything Ganttrano would bring around and looked forward to the day when, as Jonas was always promising, they'd have the chance to abuse and hold power over people.

"How about bringing a couple of those quality whores from the inn along next time you come to the farm?" Jonas teased, while Ben and Rudolf watched and listened with unsure smiles—knowing at any time the kidding could turn ugly and become violent. Ganttrano paused, taking a drag from his cigarette. "Eva goes nuts every time I give pussy away, and you sorry-ass freeloaders ain't gonna give me a nickel or tip the chicks, then I'll also have two pissed-off girls to deal with." Jonas laughed. "I buy enough shit from you, I should have your daughter!" Ganttrano countered, "I don't have a daughter, but if I did, she wouldn't be dealing with perverted pricks like you guys!" Now he was also laughing, kidding right back to Jonas. "And if she existed, she'd know what was good for her, she'd stay away from me, maybe give me a ten-minute phone call every Christmas day!" They were all laughing now. They didn't trust each other, or anybody for that matter, but they were laughing together, and that helped sustain what little criminal camaraderie there was.

One warm late night during early fall 1960, Jonas, drinking in the inn's barroom, told Ganttrano about his plans to develop a full-scale Nazi death camp, and that he had already started the project. "You're full of shit, Jonas. I know you're a little nuts, but you're not that goddamn nuts."

Jonas gave him a penetrating look and asked, "Wanna see?" They drove to the farm, and Ganttrano watched in shocked silence as Ben and Rudolf burned a cadaver smuggled in from the medical lab. "If you ever tell anyone about what we do here, I'll have you killed, I hope you can understand and appreciate that." Ganttrano didn't hesitate. "I don't talk, give me some fuckin credit!" Then he asked, "When are you gonna go get some live bodies—one bullet to the center of the forehead—bang!" Ben's response showed that he had given it some serious thought. "We're working on that—you're the only killer here, maybe we should ask you how it's done." Ganttrano kept his mouth shut. He understood that if these psychos do decide they want him to do some killing, it wouldn't be wise to refuse.

Jonas told him his father had wanted to kill Will not only because of his war service, but because his family had refused to help him, causing him to live all his life just barely above the level of poverty. "I've hated him since we were schoolmates, I watched my father become a tired and defeated man while Will Hartman's family enjoyed prosperity and happiness." He continued the diatribe—to Ganttrano it was obviously recited many times before. "His appointment to West Point, and all the accolades he received when he returned from the war a hero, churned up all the bad memories, but now I'm gonna settle the score—I owe that to my father."

Ganttrano listened impatiently to Jonas describe his outrage when he read the newspaper accounts of Will killing the concentration-camp commander and his assistant. He didn't want to further antagonize Jonas, but he couldn't resist setting the facts straight. "Those sons of bitches committed suicide, we didn't kill 'em. Will's all freaked out in the head because they popped their pills before we could search 'em."

Jonas never was going to believe that, and Ganttrano wasn't smart enough to know that he also became a marked man when he admitted being in the same room helping Will "murder" the Nazi officers. He was being spared for now because he was the drug supplier.

Jonas boasted to the soldiers how efficient his oven was. "We do this so we're ready to begin the party's work when the white people of this nation realize that America must be saved from the niggers, Jews, and the fuckin communists!" He began traveling to Philadelphia and Baltimore in search of drunks and winos, junkies, homeless pathetic men who had no family or friends—people who'd never be missed. They were baited with alcohol and drugs, and replaced the cadavers as his victims.

Jonas, Ben, Alfred, and Rudolf sat at the big oak kitchen table discussing how to kill the two drunks brought back from Philadelphia the night before. They hadn't built a gas chamber yet—so Jonas had to decide how to do it. "I never shot anybody, and I never thought of doing it." Ben spoke up, "Get Ganttrano to do it, he's killed enough fuckin Germans, and who knows how many civilians he used for target practice over there." Jonas didn't want Bill Ganttrano around any more than needed. "I'm not getting him to shoot anybody unless we don't have enough balls to do it ourselves, he's not part of us." When the two drunks started to sober up they came into the kitchen to get something to eat. Rudolf became annoyed being in the same room with them. "You're not getting anything to eat until you both take a bath, I smelled both of you the minute you walked in here." Ben joined in. "When is the last time you washed your ass?" Rudolf left the room briefly and when he returned he ordered the two, "Go out into the springhouse, I'll bring you something to eat." A few minutes later Jonas, Ben and Alfred heard the crack of two quick successive shots, and the three of them jumped up and ran out to the springhouse. The two men were lying on the floor bleeding from their heads. Jonas was overcome with shock, finding it hard to regain his composure—he threw up into the wash sink while Alfred just stood there shaking. Ben cried out, "Rudolf, what in the fuck have you done!" Still holding the pistol, he just stood there, staring down at the two bodies. "I did what we decided needed to be done." He laid the pistol on the windowsill and walked outside to have a cigarette. Ben stared at the two dead men—finally telling the others, "I guess we better get 'em burned."

That day marked the beginning of the real horror at the Konrad farm—Rudolf shot two innocent men in their heads, and Jonas, Ben, and Alfred burned them in the oven—it was the day that Fritz's dream and Jonas's plan became more important than people's lives. Why did they decide these two weak and harmless men should die? To these sick Nazi racists there were plenty of reasons—they were black homeless derelicts, poor, and sick—alcoholics and drug addicts, so unwashed they stank. Killing them was to practice killing certain people to achieve a better America and to establish and expand an Aryan race.

Jonas also wanted to develop a reputation for intelligence gathering. The Nazi government in America would have resistance—many enemies. Enemy spies would be everywhere, and he wanted to be given the job of finding out who they are. Alfred had soldiers dig two pits, measuring eight feet by eight feet, in back of the barn. About ten feet deep—they covered them with concrete slabs that had been used to cover two old wells—two small openings were covered with chicken wire. Jonas selected which derelicts were thrown into the pits, postponing their deaths, a rehearsal for the imprisoning and torturing of spies—getting intelligence secrets from them before they died from exposure during the sweltering heat of summer or the frigid cold of winter. The pit prisoners were never given any food, but did get water to drink when rainfall or snowfall produced puddles on the mud floors. Before their rendezvous with the oven, their agonizing moans while dying from exposure were silenced when Rudolf would shoot them. They'd beg him to do that.

Jonas and Fritz Konrad had worked long and hard for the Nazi party, and Jonas was convinced the takeover of America, with his appointment to a high-level leadership position in the new government, would all be happening in just a year or two, as soon as the Nazi leaders who fled Germany for South America got settled in, invested the foreign currency they had looted before the surrender, and began recruiting and training mercenaries.

Security is important when committing crimes against humanity, even in an out-of-the-way rural neighborhood in Pennsylvania. If the intruder happened to see, through the springhouse window, a body being placed in the oven and then tells the police, obviously there would be a murder investigation.

Ben Kaiser drove to the end of the lane and put up a sign with a message lettered in fresh red paint, "No Trespassing". Walking through the waist-high weeds, he hammered the signpost into the ground and noticed laying there a woman's brown shoe, a size that'd fit a small dainty foot. Picking it up, he knew right away its good condition meant it was only recently lost there. He threw it onto the front seat of his truck. When he returned to the farmhouse, he handed it to Jonas. "This could belong to the peeping Tom we had around here." They all concluded what everyone had suspected. Jonas said, "I'm sure that shoe belongs to our little friend from the market, that little bitch that gave me and Ben such a hard time."

Ben volunteered to confront her. "Let me take her the shoe, I'll ask her what she was looking for and what she saw when she looked in the window." Jonas shook his head in amazement, reminded that his organization needed more members who had the mental capacity to lead. He asked, "Why in the world would you do that?" Ben just shrugged his shoulders. Jonas explained, "We don't want her to suspect we know she was snooping around here, and besides, we have no idea what she actually saw." He watched Ben display disinterest in what to him was complicated but logical strategy. "Everyone was told she was sent away to tend her grandmother, but we know the real reason—the police told her parents to get her under control and reverse her destructive behavior or she'll be prosecuted for stealing your money."

Rudolf joined the discussion. "Assuming it's her shoe, we need to sit tight until she comes back, then find out what she knows. Before I shot those two bastards all they could get us for was abusing a corpse—burning bodies from the medical lab. We crossed the line now, a murder investigation means life in prison or the electric chair for all of us, and we know that we're gonna have to kill more people. On the other hand, if she does decide to go to the police we need to kill her before she tells them anything."

Jonas added, "We can't panic, she probably didn't see anything, and even if she did, remember the girl is unpredictable, there is a chance she wouldn't go to the police even if she did see something." Ben interrupted, "I think she's gonna blackmail us, she thinks we killed that corpse she saw going in the oven. She can't be trusted—if she can get some money from us, she could use it to run off with her boyfriend, the kid she isn't supposed to be fucking, the Hartman kid." Jonas felt a subtle agitation when he thought of Martha and Seth having sex, his love/hate feelings for her prompted an inkling of denial that brought about his refusal to accept Ben's premise. "The Hartman kid's got money, he don't need any money from her. He isn't going anywhere, he'll never leave the Oregon Inn because he knows he's gonna inherit it—he thinks like all greedy Hartmans."

Jonas had developed a plan he kept secret that allowed him to have everything he wanted, sex with Martha while at the same time furthering his Nazi mission. Because he knew she'd surely reject and resist him, the plan required she be forced to cooperate, and then killed after no longer needed. He'd make sure his hate for her would triumph over any infatuation he had for her, a true test of a man with the twisted beliefs and mission of horror like his. He could think of many reasons to hate her, her youth, and her innocence mixed with just a small bit of young sinning, being the lover of a half-breed, and the probability she will become a Hartman. He felt confident he could spare himself any pain of lost love as long as he forced himself to keep hating her. By promising himself to order her death he'd be doing the rejecting, denying her the chance to spurn him. However, he knew the real reason to hate her needed to be the mission, the reason to rape and impregnate her needed to be the mission, and finally the reason to kill her needed to be the mission.

He decided putting his plan to work would wait until he returned from a long planned trip back to Argentina. There he got reacquainted with Freda Koller, a German woman in her early thirties, who had moved there with her parents who fled Germany after the war. She had European beauty, with noticeably strong German features, deep blue eyes, of normal height, and with long blond hair that she wore pinned up in a twist. Jonas had met her six months earlier when he traveled to Argentina to buy weapons from Nazi exiles. He was in awe of her father, a bureaucrat in Hitler's regime.

They became lovers, and she returned to America with him. Because she was pure German of recent genealogy, not the product of generations of Americanization, he planned to begin his Aryan race by having her bear him as many children as she could. He was never gentle with her, but she never expected that. He'd only hit her occasionally—when something or somebody would upset him. She was loyal to him as if programmed by some invisible natural force. She knew there'd also be other women bearing his children. She was a devoted believer, convinced that these children that would come out of her and other women were the only hope for the human race.

However, Freda failed to conceive. After she was examined, the doctors found that she never would. Devastated, she traveled home to her parents in Argentina, living with them until her father was kidnapped and taken to Israel, along with her mother, he was to be tried for crimes against humanity. Freda was allowed to stay and apply for Argentinean citizenship, but was driven back to Jonas by the hope she'd learn to feel at home in America, and that they'd marry someday. He took her being barren in stride. It didn't matter to him which women he impregnated, as long as they met the genetic standard.

In February 1961, six months after she returned from Argentina, Jonas got Ben, Rudolf, and Freda to sit with him at the kitchen table next to the old coal and wood stove, still only heating the kitchen. He told them of his plan. "After the girl returns home, even if it's another year, Freda will become her friend, like Hannah is, but Freda will be able to become more of a confidante because she's younger and can speak German to her." Freda was not enthused about this task— and she let her opinion be known. "If you find out she saw you putting a body in the oven, what are you gonna do to her?" He answered, "Under this plan it doesn't matter what she saw that night."

Freda's reaction was not what Jonas wanted to see. She ran from the room holding her hands over her ears as he laid out the details and pronounced Martha's sentence. He had decided to build an underground dungeon in the cellar of the farmhouse, kidnap her, and imprison her there. He'd impregnate her and she'd bear his children, the beginnings of an Aryan race in America. Martha was genetically pure, her ancestors never married outside their church, they remained all German for almost two hundred fifty years. Hannah and Freda would both help with the labor and deliveries. Freda would pad her clothing, appear in public as pregnant, as the children were born, she'd raise them—the children would always know her as their mother. After Martha couldn't conceive or carry children anymore, Rudolf or Ben would kill her.

After he told them the plan that had been incubated and hatched inside his sick mind he went for a walk in the woods alone, using the solitude to commend himself for hating her and not crossing the line—allowing himself to fall in love with her would make him the fool in an impossible fantasy where she'd want to be with him—they'd get married and have their children—raping and killing her wouldn't be necessary then. It was obvious to him that Martha was responsible for her own fate.

When he returned from his walk he found Freda standing on the porch smoking a cigarette, trembling. Her hand shook as she juggled the lit cigarette to her mouth. He walked up behind her, put his hand on her shoulder, and spoke softly. She felt his warm breath on her neck. "You grew up in Germany living in the shadow of the Nazi Party, you and your mother made sacrifices so your father could work to help achieve a better world, for these reasons I trust you and count on you. Don't ever give me a reason to doubt your loyalty." She snapped her head and turned toward him, hurling a penetrating stare. She said nothing.

Chapter 10

At Orbachville, Martha's every move was controlled, and she reacted by sulking—shutting out everything and everyone, living in a private world overcast with dejection.

She missed Seth—the hurt was worse than she expected, and the separation was just one more complication threatening their relationship. For a young couple, new to serious love, it'd be easy to sidestep the hurdles and just walk away. She wanted to believe their love was strong enough, that they'd be together someday, but the tiring, beleaguered thoughts questioning how it ever was going to happen were always on her mind. She wrote to him, handing the letter personally to the mailman when nobody was watching her.

"Seth, I don't think I can live if I thought I'll never ever kiss you or feel your arms around me again. I guess we're just like Romeo and Juliet, but they had a tragic ending, I know we won't—nobody's gonna keep us apart—if you really want me, I'm yours." The love letter gave him a lift, but he too was struggling everyday with the same frustrations their relationship always brought on. "If my father knew that I was writing you, he'd make me stay here forever. I really think he's gonna disown me, and that makes me feel really bad. I know this is all very hard on my mother. Never forget that I love you now more than ever, and that I'll love you forever, I promise. Never leave me. Everything will turn out OK. I love you. Martha"

She missed her mother, father, brothers, and cousins—never being away before. Rebecca wrote her daughter each week, reminding her to cooperate and do her chores, study hard in school, attend church and say her prayers.

Many local members of the sect in Orbachville, especially the older ones, noticed her sad mood and voiced concern. She endured over and over the same question, "Why the frown, the sad blue eyes, the tears—all spoiling such a pretty face?" Her lips, moistened by warm salted tears, had a few of the older men wishing she were a much younger little girl so they could taste them. They remained decent though, giving appropriate comfort to a young woman, settling for a hug, holding her hand, or perhaps even kissing her forehead like the mentoring women did. She wanted to tell them all to leave her alone. She resisted striking out—screaming to everyone to mind their own business. She knew they wouldn't really understand, even if she could sort everything out in her mind and explain her feelings to anyone. She cried herself to sleep every night.

Her grandmother, Sally Dern, and her Aunt Julia Kline, were very religious, their lives revolved around the sect's church. Now that Martha was a member of their household, she was required to participate in daily prayer, attend church Wednesday and Saturday nights and three church services on Sunday—a daily life that fulfilled her father's blueprint for her redemption.

Sally was a short and small-featured elderly woman, her long thin gray hair pinned up and tucked under her bonnet. Age had made her frail, but when she talked about her faith, she transformed into a strong-willed and vocal firebrand, admonishing anyone within earshot of the consequences of falling from righteousness. Grandfather Dern had died many years earlier from a farming accident.

Aunt Julia was a middle-aged woman, in her late thirties, who at one time was quite beautiful. Her looks were mature—long brown hair under her bonnet, her brown eyes helped by wire rimmed eyeglasses that made her look older than she really was. She had been married years ago—her husband left for work one morning and never came back. She had a grown son who moved away as soon as he graduated from school. Julia was envious of her young, smart and beautiful niece— she was everything she could've been if she would have worked harder in school and not fallen in love and married the boy that eventually became a lazy and irresponsible man.

Martha was also required to attend activities of the church's youth group—forbidden to attend any social events outside the church community. Many of the boys were smitten over her, but she reacted with indifference—during the summer weeks before school started up again she already got a reputation as a snob.

After a youth prayer meeting she met Emily Snyder, who introduced herself as her new schoolteacher for the 1960-61 school term. She wasn't Brethren—she didn't wear a bonnet— she mostly wore long sleeve blouses and skirts reaching just below the knee. Emily was a pretty twenty-six-year-old spinster with short chestnut brown hair, brown eyes, and a pretty face with a milky white complexion. Some would call her homely, but she was too pretty to be that. She never wore make-up.

All this surprised and fascinated Martha. Emily wasn't hired to teach the sect's religion or rigid way of life, she was signed on as a regular schoolteacher because her education qualified her for the state certification the sect needed to operate the school. "I'll also be counseling you, we'll be starting our sessions next week." Sitting with Martha by the piano in the church activity hall, she asked her how she was handling the changes in her life. "I hate it here, I hate these people, I hate my grandmother, I hate my Aunt Julia." Emily's response was calm and quiet. "Hate is a terrible emotion, it consumes you, it can destroy you." Martha knew all that—she had been preached to about hate from the time she was a little girl. "I think these church people—they're hypocrites, they feel they're qualified to judge me, the Bible says that it's wrong to judge other people, but they do it anyway."

"I had a long telephone conversation with your mother, she told me all about your problems. Your mother loves you very much, she's known for some time that you're a special child, she described you as a very bright girl who hides her gentle and sincere inner self with a rough and tough outer shell." She waited for Martha's reaction. "My mother would be my closest friend if it wasn't for her devotion to the church. The elders tell her that she must honor and obey my father, that she's the garden where her husband sows his seed." She seemed to be making excuses for her, not wanting to admit she'd probably put the church ahead of her children. "She always felt guilty when she gave me extra time—more time than most children get, knowing it was time taken away from my father."

At first, as expected, Martha didn't trust Emily, but she warmed to her mostly because she wasn't a sect member. The first two counseling sessions were tense, but Emily was confident they'd start a dialogue. She convinced Martha that whatever they talked about would remain confidential.

The sessions continued the rest of summer—Martha slowly began opening up, they met two or three times a week in the church conference room. She believed the root cause of her problems was being a member of a conservative Brethren family, very confining to a girl with a rebellious nature who wanted to learn a profession, travel, have adventures, and never stop learning. Emily learned one of Martha's ambitions was to become a detective—solve mysteries and help bring people to justice. She finally admitted to someone that she trespassed on the Konrad farm one night, giving Emily the first hint of the story yet to come. She felt relieved telling somebody a short version of her experience, now that she was confident Emily would help her deal with the horrible encounter when she felt comfortable enough to relive the whole story.

Often they'd eat their lunch at a picnic table in the church grove. "When we talk at lunch, is that part of my counseling, or is it because we're friends?" Emily explained, "When we talk—wherever we talk—we talk as Emily and Martha. Let's just say we have a special relationship."

Martha said, "I've never had anybody I could really talk to, explain how I felt about different things until I met Seth— he'd listen for hours, he never criticizes me or tries to boss me around and tell me what to do, at least most of the time. That's why I love him." Emily responded with a hard question. "But does he really love you?" Martha replied, "He told me he did, and I believe him. We were gonna go all the way but I wanted to wait until we get married." She was telling her things she never thought she'd tell a schoolteacher.

Emily's priority was to gain Martha's trust and to keep it. "Don't forget, you can talk to me about anything you want to talk about—it won't go any further than here." Instead of criticizing her for her past behavior—taking her clothing off with a boy, smoking and drinking, Emily gave her a compliment. "You showed you're responsible by not getting pregnant, it would have made things worse—hurting your family, and perhaps Seth would have felt rushed or trapped."

Martha spelled out the grim certainty. "When they finally concede that I'm gonna be with him, my father will disown me, he'll never accept Seth." Emily was dismayed when she heard her say that. "It's hard for me to believe that. I think he'll eventually accept him as your husband." Martha now was beginning to lose patience with her mentor. "He'll never accept it, never, don't you understand English? He'll refuse to recognize our marriage or acknowledge my children as his grandchildren—that's what I'll have to learn to live with. I won't care when the church shuns me, that's bad enough, but it's not near as bad as the Amish, and I can accept my family shunning me, but it's gonna really hurt to have my father not only shun me, but disown me, to wish he hadn't fathered me." She paused—the strained look on her face was obvious. "Do I deserve that type of treatment from my own father?" Emily sighed, suspecting solving Martha's problems was going to be a long struggle. "No, you don't, but remember you must live your own life, do what you feel is the right thing for you." It wasn't what Emily was being paid to tell her.

After church services, as the churchgoers were standing about on a warm and bright August Sunday, Emily approached Sally and Julia who were standing with Martha. "Would it be OK if Martha spent a couple hours with me at my house to help me get my papers ready for school to reopen?" Aunt Julia was quick to give reasons she couldn't. "She has to help with dinner, and she has her other work to do." Sally intervened. "She can help, but she must be home in a little while."

As they drove to Emily's house, Martha reacted. "You see what I have to deal with, 'In a little while,' what does that mean? One hour, two hours, ten hours, what?" Emily laughed, seeking some humor in it all as the girl complained. Then Martha blurted out, "Are you a lesbian?" She didn't pause—too uneasy, even scared, to wait for an answer. "I don't care if you are, I just don't want that to be the reason you're helping me." Emily pulled the car off to the side of the road. The difficult girl had tired the teacher many times, and now despite keeping her cool yet another time, she was feeling more anger than usual. "How about if I take you home, maybe I made a mistake trying to help you?" She was beginning to think she was getting too close to her. "I thought you and I had developed some mutual trust, a friendship that you desperately need." Emily also needed this developing friendship. "I wasn't raised in this church—I joined it to get this job. I told them I believe in everything they do, but that's not true. I lied because I felt if I got the job I could help kids, even kids like you." Martha had never heard her raise her voice before. "But you can be a very ungrateful child, you're very capable of hurting people, but you're not going to hurt me!" Martha was crying now, trying her best to talk while sniffling to hold back more tears. "I'm sorry, I feel like I can't trust anyone." Emily answered, "I hope once and for all you can come to trust me." Martha responded, "I trust you, and I need your help, please don't lose faith in me or stop helping me." Emily put the car back on the road. "Make sure you address me as Miss Snyder in school, not Emily, our relationship is supposed to be professional only. And no, I'm not a lesbian, but even if I was that wouldn't be the reason I'd be helping you or being your teacher."

Life got a little better when school started in September. She had written her mother telling her she was anxious to start school and earn good grades. The real reason she was glad to start school was to get time away from Sally and Julia.

The Dern's mailbox sat on a post along Mexico Road, easy for Ben Kaiser to rifle it every day watching for a letter from Martha. Finally he had her address without the family's knowledge. Convinced that the girl was a threat, capable of blackmailing him and the others at the Konrad farm, he decided to disobey Jonas. Despite knowing the punishment meted out by Jonas would be swift and severe if he was found out, Ben planned to visit her and find out for himself what she knew.

The Orbachville School had six classrooms and a total of about 180 students in grades 1 to 12. The first day of her senior year, Martha met classmate Elizabeth Martin, who lived just down the road from Sally Dern's house. Martha was a leader—Elizabeth, like Naomi, was a follower. She had always wanted to be the best friend of the prettiest girl in school, and Martha, the new girl, was the prettiest one in school by far. Elizabeth wore thick glasses, her hair in pigtails coiled up under her bonnet. She was skinny and slightly pigeon-toed, but also smart, a good cook, and very proficient at housework and attending to her younger brothers and sisters, nieces, and nephews.

Martha right away took advantage of Elizabeth's admiration and devotion. She convinced her to steal mystery books at the drugstore and had her spy for her—she wanted to know who was talking nice about her or "stabbing her in the back". Elizabeth's reward was a chance to become popular and be accepted by association. Martha was always able to convince people they were her best friends. She'd turn on her charm and then demand and get unwavering loyalty.

Elizabeth considered Martha a bad girl, in awe when she talked about her life before moving to Orbachville, telling her about Seth and his family and the Oregon Inn. She fascinated her with stories about their hideaway. Elizabeth asked, "Did you do it with him?" Martha answered, "What makes you think I'd tell you if I did?" They laughed. "We never went all the way, we decided to wait until we get married. But now I wish we had." Elizabeth was also a good friend because she'd tell Martha what she wanted to hear. She confided, "The church says we aren't supposed to do that with a boy, but I know how much you love him, it just can't be bad to be in love like that!" Martha added, "I guess at our age, he and I shouldn't be so serious, so much could go wrong, but he has his future planned because his family has provided him with opportunity—but he's gonna change things at the inn as soon as he's old enough— he isn't gonna wait until he inherits it before he puts the Hartman family back in charge. His dream is for me and him to get married, run the inn, and raise a family."

The elders of the church, along with Martha's parents, grandmother, aunt, as well as Emily and Miriam Kistler, a fifty-six year old serious and no nonsense teacher, also state certified, were all charged with providing positive influences on Martha's development, molding her into a God-fearing, pious young woman to become a devoted wife, mother, and church worker, no longer possessing her sinful thinking and desires. Except for Emily, and now Elizabeth, all these people were unaware of her relationship with Seth. If any of them found out the details, she knew they'd make it impossible for her to be in contact with him, even by letter.

On the Monday morning that started the third week of the school term, Mrs. Kistler and Emily announced that money had been stolen from the locked filing cabinet in the rear of the classroom. The kids all turned to the back and saw how the cabinet was pried open, the top drawer twisted and bent. "Thirty dollars has been stolen—if any student knows who took the money, they need to report them to me," Mrs. Kistler said.

Martha now considered herself an amateur private detective and wanted to solve this crime. She had already figured out who the worst among the worse boys in her class were.

After two days and nobody coming forward, Martha told Elizabeth she was going to solve the crime. "I'm gonna need an assistant, do you wanna help?" Elizabeth, anxious to please her only friend and have the opportunity to be important, was surprised Martha would let her help solve a crime. "We're gonna set a trap, I'm gonna be the bait. You just make sure you keep your mouth shut, if you tell anybody what we're doing, it'll blow the case." That night the two girls discussed the plan—going over all the details. Elizabeth reassured Martha. "I'm scared and nervous, but you can trust me, I'm gonna do this."

The next day Elizabeth told the three boys Martha thought might be the guilty ones that Martha would be willing to take off her clothing for any boy that was willing to pay $10. She told them Martha's made-up story. "Consider yourself lucky. She needs to send her boyfriend money that he owes gangsters." Despite being taught lying was a sin, Elizabeth was admittedly having fun—making the story very dramatic, almost unbelievable to anyone but the three naïve boys. "If he doesn't pay 'em back, they're going to beat him up, or maybe even kill him. That's how gangsters operate, he's been begging Martha to send him money." The boys were excited, asking when and where this was all going to take place. Elizabeth said, "She'll do it in the woods in back of the school right after class tomorrow." Elizabeth hurried to Martha's house and whispered the details to her—"the boys would be there"—as they sat on the porch swing. Martha, speaking very quietly to prevent someone overhearing, said, "You certainly have a flair for the dramatic!" Elizabeth's face lit up with a big smile, showing proud appreciation for the compliment, but it quickly changed to a fearful frown. "Did I go too far?" Martha said, "Well, evidently not, they believed you. Remember, they're not the smartest guys in the world." They both laughed, then Elizabeth asked, "They're very excited about all this, the thought of seeing you naked is driving 'em crazy. What are you gonna do when they expect you to get undressed?" She answered, "That's a good question, I might have to do it. For me that's no big deal, in fact it's sort of thrilling when I think of doing that." That night, as she lay in bed trying to go to sleep, she thought about how the story naïve Elizabeth feared was overfilled with fantasy could very easily become reality if Seth really did succumb to the temptations of organized crime, only then she'd have to do a lot more with her body than just show it to a bunch of goggling men.

She never forgot that Seth was living in a criminal environment that was vicious and brutal. That's why their hideaway was such an important place—they could be alone to do whatever they wanted, while keeping him away from the inn and its wicked goings-on, even if only for a few hours at a time. But now that she was away she feared he could very well become a victim of the racketeering surrounding him, or worse, be tempted to become a mobster like his Uncle Sal. These anxious thoughts, fueled by being lovesick, just added to the stress of being sent away.

The next day Martha and Elizabeth were waiting when Jason Horst and two classmates, Bryan and David, showed up. Jason was Martha's chief suspect—she had kept that to herself. He was a good-looking muscular farm boy with a crew cut, always being chased by girls, always serious, he was a fighter. She told Elizabeth to collect $10 from each boy.

Jason warned, "This better not be a goddamn trick or I'll beat your ass." He didn't scare her—she was threatened before. "You're a real tough guy," unable to resist putting him in his place. "You'd think a little boy who'd like to be a man would be anxious to see a naked girl, and not be making threats." Jason sneered, "I don't get worked up to see a whore's tits and pussy, and that's what you are. I know all about you." Now his cruel remarks were bothering her, but she kept quiet, she was getting too nervous to respond now that the time to "put up or shut up" had arrived. He kept taunting her. "Your Italian stallion mobster boyfriend isn't here to protect you now, so do what you're being paid to do." Elizabeth was frenzied, nervously looking up at the school for signs of any adults as she collected the money. Needing to keep the upper hand, Martha ridiculed the boys still more, "You three have never seen a naked girl before, have you?" Bryan said, "I didn't come here to be made fun of, just show me your pussy." She asked, "Where did you get the $10, Bryan, you never have any money, and what about you, David, where did you get $10." David gave away the secret. "Jason's paying for all of us." Jason yelled, "Shut up, David, it's none of her business who's paying!" Martha reacted, "Jason, I'm impressed, you're the money guy, and you're willing to share your riches with your friends." He ignored her insults— hiding his own nervousness by shouting, "We're ready, quit stalling, pull your pants down!"

Chapter 11

She was standing in back of a tree trying to kindle enough courage to unbutton her dress when a surly and boorish voice came out of the thick brush. "Must I pay $10 too, or do people you ripped off get a free look?" Startled, she looked toward the voice and saw Ben Kaiser standing there, despicable grin on his face, a flaunted painted still life of hate. Elizabeth panicked—she put the $30 in Martha's hand and ran out of the woods followed by Bryan and David. Jason stood there overwhelmed, unable to move—he had never faced an adult threatening violence before. Then, never taking his eyes off Kaiser, he slowly walked over to Martha. Her eyes were affixed to the villain as well. "Jason, leave, this doesn't concern you. I'll be all right." He knew they were in a serious 'fight-or-flee' situation.

He was trying to figure Kaiser out: gangster, kidnapper, sexual predator—whoever and whatever he was, he knew he was evil. Martha yelled, "Jason, leave!" Ben, still wearing the grin, gave the same advice. "You better leave, boy, she's a powder keg, not someone to reckon with. You're much better off to follow the cute little thing's orders." Jason turned and walked toward the school. When he was out of sight she asked Ben, "What do you want, what are you doing here?" Now his grin was gone—he had a very serious look as he walked toward her. She walked backward trying to stay away from his reach but tripped on a large fallen tree limb and fell down. He reached down and grabbed her by the throat, lifting her up off the ground with just one of his large, hairy, muscular arms. He had a strong offensive smell of sweat, and as he pulled her face up against his, she could smell his unwashed hair and his cigarette breath, made worse by his yellowed, filthy teeth.

"Are you gonna spit in my face now? I dare you to give me a reason to beat you to death." She couldn't respond—she was choking from his hand around her throat, her feet still not touching the ground. He kept yelling at her. "Why were you snooping around the farmhouse, looking in the windows?" He didn't wait for her to respond. "I wanna know what you saw, I wanna know who sent you there, don't play games with me girl, I wanna hear some answers." She started swinging her arms, then put both her hands on the one of his that was wrapped around her throat, digging her fingernails in it while trying to peel it off her throat. He let her drop and grabbed her hair, swinging her around into a headlock. She yelled, "I was just out for a walk, and I didn't see anything. Let me alone!" Releasing her from the headlock, he threw her to the ground, and dropped to his knees, straddling her and putting one of his knees against her chest to hold her down. She launched a vicious defense, screaming, spitting in his face, and trying to scratch his face. He used one hand to hold her wrists to the ground above her head and slapped her with the back of his other hand. The slap cut her lip—the blood gushing and streaming down her chin onto her dress. He pulled up her dress and yanked down her panties, almost at the same time unbuttoning his trousers. Now she stopped resisting, her screaming became instead tearful sobbing as she realized that she was about to be violated, her earlier confident thoughts about how to react to this situation now vanished. As he prepared to go inside her, he said, "You better not be lying to me, cause I'll kill you." He was surprised that she stopped fighting. "Now you're proving what I've always said, you want a real man to take you and make you a woman, when I'm finished you won't be a little girl anymore."

He wasn't smart enough to protect himself. Martha regained some of her strength and started to resist again, flailing her arms and kicking her legs as much as she could with his weight on top of her. She squirmed underneath him, inching just enough to one side where her right leg was between his legs. He tried to adjust himself, but before he could, she jerked her knee up into his groin with all the strength she could muster. He rolled off her, doubled up in pain. He uttered while in agony, "You bitch, you dirty little goddamn bitch!" She sat up, trying to get to her feet, but she couldn't. She crawled away as fast as anyone could with a back in pain from such a fall, a bruised face, scraped knees, and bleeding mouth.

Jason heard early on stories about cowards, and he read about them. His father, brothers, and uncles always said there isn't anything worse than having a coward in the family. He came back knowing if he didn't defend Martha from the evil stranger he'd become one, and with that branding he'd spend his whole life at odds with himself. When he saw her sitting on the ground spitting blood from her cut lip, and Ben staggering to his feet trying to recover from his agony, he hit him in the face with his fist, knocking him back to the ground. He tried to stand up again, getting only to his knees, and Jason hit him again. Ben fell down on his back, bleeding from his mouth and nose, unconscious.

Jason grabbed her hand, pulling her along, both running as fast as they could until they got to the woods near his house, only two miles from the school and about a mile from Sally Dern's. Out of breath, both uncomfortable with their injuries, his hand was throbbing, the pain made it feel like it was broken from its impact with Kaiser's face. They stayed hidden for more than an hour until nightfall—there was always a chance Ben Kaiser was following them.

She told him, "I'm gonna return the money to Mrs. Kistler, but I'm not gonna tell her where I got it, I owe you that for coming back to help me." She thought more of him now—she never thought he'd come back. "You don't need to steal, Jason, you're a good person or you wouldn't have cared what happened to me, and good people don't steal."

Luckily Sally and Julia were away when she got home, making it easier for her to clean herself up and treat her wounds. A scared Elizabeth showed up, becoming hysterical when she saw Martha's bruised face and her pained walk. Martha calmed her down. "Stop carrying on, everything's fine, don't worry about that guy, just help me get cleaned up, I have to hide the cuts and black and blue marks." They stuffed her torn and soiled dress and underpants into the kitchen coal stove, watching them burn up in seconds. "Jason came back and saved me, I'm not gonna turn him in, or Bryan or David. I'm gonna give Mrs. Kistler the money and we're all gonna pretend it never happened." Martha was content knowing she solved the crime, convinced she could become a good detective. She warned Elizabeth, "Don't forget, it never happened, and don't say a word about it to nobody, and I mean nobody. Do you understand?" Elizabeth nodded—she'd do whatever Martha asked.

She had to hide bruises on her body and conceal the soreness and pain. None of it was that difficult for a strong-minded girl. Her long-sleeved dresses with low hemlines, and knee high socks covered up the bruises. Her cut lip was explained away as the result of a fall. It was especially hard to hide the back pain, but after a few days she was OK.

She went to Mrs. Kistler and Emily and gave them the $30. She told them the person who stole it gave it to her, and is sorry for stealing it, she never mentioned Jason. That afternoon Jason confessed, and to Martha's dismay, he told them the whole story—why he gave Martha the money, that this strange man attacked her, she tried to defend herself, and that he came back to fetch her and wound up hitting and knocking the attacker out cold. Later the two teachers would learn a lot more, but the only part of the story Emily believed initially was Jason stealing the money. In addition to his parent's punishment, he was required to write a letter of apology to the school, undergo counseling with Emily, and spend weeks doing service work for the school and church.

When school was finished that day, Emily told Martha she'd drive her home. "I'm afraid I'm going to have to tell your grandmother and aunt what you did. I have no idea how much of Jason's story is true, or how much you and him concocted, but I do know if you were willing to tempt a boy with sex and take off your clothing for money, you have bigger problems than I suspected."

Martha figured there wasn't anything she could say or do to get out of the current mess she was in, but it was but a snag compared to her real troubles. She doubted anybody would believe the real story, and Ben Kaiser would now probably kill her when he gets the opportunity.

Sally Dern listened as Emily told her what her granddaughter had done while trying to solve a crime, and how some strange man supposedly became attracted to her, stalked her, and assaulted her. Sally knew what punishment to order. "You're grounded for a month except to go to school, and there's gonna be extra housework." Aunt Julia joined in. "I don't know what's gonna become of you, taking your clothing off in front of three boys! And who is this older man who came to see you? Where did you meet him? Weak men wanna have sex with young girls when they're teased and tempted by immoral women—did you ever have sex with this man? If you did you're a whore!" She didn't let up, or give Martha any chance to respond. "You've always ignored everything you've been taught at home and in church. Girl, you need to pray for salvation!"

Martha, finally having enough, began shouting, "You're not gonna treat me like this anymore, I've been expected to do most the cleaning and cooking around here like a hired maid, and then I'm accused of doing all these terrible things here and back home. Well, not anymore!" She stormed out of the house while Sally, Julia and Emily stood there in silence.

The next day in school Emily told her, "Even though I don't agree with what you did and were prepared to do, I do appreciate that you got the school's money back. There's still time for Jason to be helped, and justice was served." Martha said, "I know I can be a problem, but I did what I thought needed to be done, sometimes I forget what people are gonna think." Emily put her arms around her and gave her a hug. "You're a sweet girl, but trouble always seems to find you. I'm worried about you."

In May Sally Dern died, and Aunt Julia decided to move to Wisconsin to be close to her son and his wife and children. On the day she was set to leave she set aside just a few minutes for Martha. "Until the school term ends you'll be staying in the home of church members, then you'll be sent back home to your parents, you'll be able to lie around with that Italian kid again, at least until your father finds out." Martha, forced to submit to Julia's disdain ever since she came to Orbachville, suspected that her aunt wanted a last chance showdown, and now she was prepared to stand and fight. "Why don't you tell him all about it, all the bad things I do? You seem to want him to know, that way you can hurt me, but remember, you'll also be hurting him. Is that what you want?" Her twisted face, with curled lip, had been distorted by her contempt for the young girl, but now it relaxed. She fell silent, the snarl leaving her voice

"I'm not gonna tell him, I should've done a long time ago what you're gonna do—fight to be with someone who really cares about you. You have more guts than I ever had, you'll break away, it's too late for me." Martha, these awkward moments making her feel uncomfortable, finally responded, "You're gonna move away and be with your son, that's breaking away." Julia laughed. "My son is more Brethren than your father, he supports our small sect more than even your grandmother did. I'm going to him because I have no place else to go, I have to plan for the day when I become old and helpless." Amazingly, Martha was trying to comfort this woman who caused her so much anguish. "Maybe you'll meet someone, a man you can marry." Julia offered a slight smile. "Look at me, no man is ever gonna want me, I have to face the facts, deal with reality. I tried making your life miserable because I was jealous of you. I wanna apologize for that. I'm sorry." They both flinched from the car horn honking from the driveway. A lone tear fell down Julia's cheek as she cautiously walked close to Martha. With all the emotional strength Martha could muster she put her arms around her aunt and kissed her on the neck. She picked up Julia's suitcase and handed it to the deacon waiting at the door, and then watched her get into the car taking her to the airport. She looked around the big kitchen, once a center of activity, the smell of food frying and baking, German and English talk of the goings-on in the community and the world, all the senses gone to the past now. She slowly walked from room to room—she had never seen the big house like this before, so dark and quiet, it was as if its spirit died when Sally Dern did.

Martha expected Emily would volunteer to take her in. A church elder brought the good news—she'd be staying with Emily until it was time for her to return home to her parents.

Happy to be out of her grandmother's house and the strict controls, she was also apprehensive about moving back home. It had been a long, terrible year. She was prepared for the worse—maybe Seth met another girl and didn't want her anymore.

She had witnessed something very horrible when she spied at the Konrad farm. Being away had given her a chance to delay dealing with it, but it was always on her mind, she hid her nightmares about it from everyone, even when Ben Kaiser's assault and threats caused them to get worse.

She awoke screaming, shaking, her heart racing, the terror of reliving those moments, experiencing shock and disgust when she looked through the farmhouse window, then running home and climbing back through her bedroom window, sweaty, out of breath. Emily heard the screams and ran to her—kneeling at her bed. She reached for a tissue and dabbed the perspiration from her forehead and above her lips. "Do you want to talk about it, tell me what the nightmare was about?" Now, for the first time, Martha lost control and became hysterical. Emily was very concerned, she held her tightly until she settled down. "I think I'm in danger, I know you're not gonna believe me, but it's the truth!" Emily took her to her bedroom and held her until she finally dozed off, exhausted from the harrowing dream. They both slept late in each other's arms.

They talked for quite a while at the breakfast table. "If you're having nightmares, and if they're so vivid you're remembering them in the morning, you need to tell someone about them, whether it's me or some other professional." Emily had never seen so much fear and confusion on someone's face before. "If I tell you things, are you gonna believe me?" Emily reassured her. "I'm going to believe you, I promise."

She was prepared to listen to more of the same problems, probably exaggerated, she heard since they met—fear of losing her boyfriend and the lovesickness that goes with that, mobsters influencing him, and of course the frustration of not wanting a life that evolved from her upbringing with its harsh church and family rules. In their place she heard a story that scared her real bad, a story about a closed community of Nazis, members of the Ku Klux Klan, and radical and violent racists, very unlike the traditional Italian-immigrant organized-crime family that was part of Seth's life.

Martha began her story—"One night, actually very early in the morning, about 2 AM, I crawled out of my bedroom through the open window, and walked to the Konrad farm where this creepy guy named Jonas Konrad lives. He owns the Nazi war souvenir booth at the market. I was curious what went on there, and because I wanna be a detective, I felt this was good practice." Emily watched Martha's mood turning progressively more serious. Emily was fast coming to believe the unfolding story was not a make-believe tale. Martha continued, "I got to the farmhouse and climbed on top of a metal barrel and looked into the only window that was lit up." She stopped telling the story and ran into the living room, throwing herself across the couch, drowning her head into the overstuffed pillow. Emily, always patient, waited a few minutes before following her. "Tell me the whole story." Martha turned over, her eyes open wide but with rapid eye movement as if she were asleep, her imagination projecting across the bedroom ceiling a panorama of recalled horror. "I saw 'em put this dead body in an oven, smoke was coming out of the chimney. Just as they closed the oven door, I slipped and fell off the barrel—the noise caused the dogs to start barking. I ran as fast as I could up the lane, and just as I turned right to start down Mexico Road toward my house, I lost my one shoe, I couldn't see where it went. I tried to run, but I could only hop along because the stones on the road were jabbing my bare foot. When I got to my house I crawled back in the window and slipped into bed, I was sweating and out of breath, totally exhausted."

Emily stared ahead silently—she was scared just hearing about it, certainly a young girl that lived the experience would be a lot more so. "Did you go back and look for your shoe?" Martha answered, "I went back a few days later, I was scared to go before that. I spent a long time looking for it, I searched every inch of the area—it wasn't there." She went on with the story. "That night as I was running out the lane to Mexico Road, this Nazi, Ben Kaiser, came out of the farmhouse and raced his pickup truck up the lane like a wild man, shining his spotlight around looking for whoever got the dogs barking. I dropped to the ground and hid in the high weeds." She hadn't told anyone about this before now, but in her head she recalled every detail, every sight, sound, and smell, minute by minute, etched in her consciousness as if the devil himself put it there to haunt her. "I stayed hidden until he went back inside. That's when I got up and started running again, that's when I tripped and lost my shoe." Emily was thinking fast, hopeful the searching for a solution to the terrible dilemma would temper her own fears.

She dreaded asking Martha the obvious question—she got the answer she expected but surely didn't want. "Do you think he came back looking for clues and found your shoe?" Martha gave the shocking answer. "He definitely found my shoe, and because that convinced him I was the one who was doing the spying, he came here to Orbachville and stalked me." Emily concluded the whole story was so bizarre it had to be true, she only hoped Martha was telling her everything. "He came out of the woods while I was doing that stupid thing with the three boys. After the boys and Elizabeth ran off he attacked me, warning me if I ever open my mouth, he'll kill my family and me. I got a chance to fight back, and that's when Jason came back and hit him twice and knocked him out. That's how I got away."

Emily stressed the urgency to report everything to the police. Martha reacted firmly, "No way! I have a plan, and I'm not going to the police until I can prove there is a link between these creeps and the crooks running the Oregon Inn. The police don't know anything about what's going on at the farmhouse— they won't raid the farm without me reporting what I saw. When I do tell 'em they'll know right away they need my eyewitness testimony to get a search warrant and prosecute the case, especially if they don't find any bodies when they raid the place. I need to get more information to carry out my plan." Emily yelled, "Martha! You can't be serious—you're talking like a crime detective!" Emily was frantic. "These people aren't going to let a sixteen-year-old girl get the best of them—they'll destroy you!" Martha revealed some more details. "Bill Ganttrano, the sleazy manager of the inn, is a drug dealer—he sells drugs to these people. He's the missing link in the chain that connects the Konrad farm and the Oregon Inn. Until I can prove they're all working together, I'm not telling nobody anything—I can save the inn for Seth and his family only if I have information I can barter."

Emily shouted some more. "Have it your way! I was told that the community you come from, along this Mexico Road, was idyllic! That's not how you're describing it now!" Martha replied, "Alton Manor is like a lot of communities, idyllic on the surface, but underneath there's sick people doing sick things."

Emily, convinced Martha wasn't going to change her mind about going to the police, was determined to protect her, even if it was from herself. "I think you should go on a church mission, the only real option open to you, a calling from the church that's more important than you returning right away to your parents. It's not safe for you to go back home. This man is going to come back looking for you here, or he's going to wait for you back home, and he's going to hurt you." Martha responded candidly, "Hurt me? I wish that was the worst of it—believe me, he's gonna kill me!" Up until then Emily couldn't imagine Martha, or anyone else she knew for that matter, being murdered—but now the realness of it set in—it was like a cold dark cloud hovering over both of them, getting ready to come down like a black fog to suffocate them. She was scared—really scared.

Martha had in the past, while growing up, resisted going on church missions, but fear made her see the value in doing that very thing now. "OK, I'll go, but they'll just check with the church and find out where I am—won't they?" Emily reassured her. "I know this pastor who runs a small mission program supported by a few small sects, including the one you belong to. If I explain to him that you're in danger he'll send you away and make sure nobody knows where you are. This'll buy us some time."

Emily wanted to make sure Martha understood the importance of keeping all this under wraps. "Saving you means not telling anyone where you are, not your parents, your brothers, not even Seth." She noticed the increasing despair on her face. "When I meet with your parents to get their written permission to send you off, I'll make sure they know to mail you at the mission office in Philadelphia—your mail will be forwarded to you wherever you are because you'll be moving around a lot." Emily was sure careful planning could provide Martha with adequate protection. "We need to make sure Jonas Konrad and his people don't find out where you are, I suspect they have the resources—they know people everywhere in the world who'll destroy anyone for them, even a young girl! They'll never find you through the mission office—all information about the missionaries is well guarded—never given out."

Martha said, "He's gonna be angry—he's gonna consider this me leaving him." Emily countered, "Not if you explain to him that the church and your parents have decided to send you away to live in a hut in South America for a year, and you have no choice in the matter. Make sure you don't tell him about Ben Kaiser traveling to Orbachville and attacking you, because he'll go after him to retaliate." Martha agreed. "I know he'd do that, get arrested for assault and blow the whole case." Emily wasn't happy to hear her phrase it in the context of a detective solving a crime, "blow the whole case". The scenario was very real, not a young girl's flight of the imagination— pretending to be living amongst the pages of a paperback detective novel.

Emily contacted Pastor Leroy Johnson in Philadelphia the very next day and explained to him the details of the crisis, asking him for his help. He told her to bring Martha to Philadelphia the next day.

Three days later Martha was in Guatemala.

Chapter 12

Seth had exchanged letters with Martha infrequently while she was living in Orbachville—her latest letter telling him she was going further away. He was angry, convinced she'd rather go on a mission than come home to him. He wasn't exhibiting good character, supporting his girlfriend while she did what she needed to do. Most young men in love, finding themselves in this state of affairs, would behave the same way Seth did— he was lonely—he missed her, and he wanted her with him.

A few weeks later Emily came to the Oregon Inn—slowly walking up to the bar. Noticing nervously that all the eyes in the room were fixed on her, she asked the bartender where she could find Seth Hartman. "If he's here, he's upstairs in his room, but you can't go up there." Katie, who happened to come out of the kitchen wiping her hands on her apron, noticed the young handsome woman, a pleasant and different sight in the barroom. "Can I help you?" Emily felt more at ease when she saw the older woman with the looks of goodness. "I'm Martha Dern's school teacher, and I have a message for Seth from her." Katie, happy to hear this news, showed Emily to a table in the dining room. "I'm Seth's grandmother, I'll go get him."

When he walked into the room she stood up quickly. She realized right away that Martha's description of him was accurate, tall and handsome, classic features and a full head of black hair. "Seth, I'm Emily Snyder, Martha's schoolteacher. She asked me to come see you and tell you that the church decided after her grandmother died to send her on a church mission." He wasn't happy at all talking about it. "She sent me a letter and told me, why is she sending you around, why didn't she come home to visit before leaving?" Emily knew she had to soothe the boy's feelings even though she couldn't tell him the whole story—she couldn't very well tell him Martha would be risking her life if she came to see him. He was in love and he was feeling rejected. "Seth, I can understand that you're not happy with the way this is being handled, but let me assure you that she had no choice in the matter, the church leaders make their decisions, and that's it." She was twisting the facts, blaming the church instead of the threat from Ben Kaiser—she couldn't give him any reason to suspect she was in danger. "She hopes to be home in a year. She'll be moving around South America helping emergency hunger and medical care programs. She'd like you to write, she'll answer all your letters." Emily gave him the mission's address. "Her mail won't be censored and it'll be promptly forwarded to her unopened."

He was clearly agitated. He sat at the table—leaning back in his chair with his arms crossed, and listened to her some more, but soon cut her off, quickly sitting front and looking at the floor. "I'll write, I appreciate you coming here, give her my best." Emily waited for his eyes to meet hers, and then asked, "Can I tell her you said you love her?" He slowly stood up, buying time while thinking of a carefully worded message that'd keep intact his youthful male pride. "You can tell her that, you can also tell her it's the end for us—there's just too many people and things working against us." Emily came close to losing her composure, and she knew that'd cause irreparable damage. "Seth, if I give her that message she'll be devastated. I hope you won't tell her that when you write to her, maybe you shouldn't write to her at all. You're going to break her heart." Emily was trying to end her visit status quo, buying still more time for Martha. "Instead, wait until she comes home, give her a chance to make the decisions she has to make that will affect her life." Seth's voice bristled. "She already told me she was gonna spend her life with me, who's talked her out of that?" Emily wanted to leave now, talking was just upsetting him more—he was bitter and frustrated. "Her brothers are married now and having kids, building houses on the Dern farm, the way I see it she'll be having her kids and pleasing her husband in a house just a few hundred yards from her parents'." Emily, choosing silence—stood up and put out her hand, and when their hands met she walked to him and put her arms around him briefly. Gently backing away, she turned to Katie and nodded—hoping she could keep her grandson on track for a while, just long enough for everything to turn out OK. As she drove along Mexico Road to the main road she smiled with sadness. Now she knew why Martha was in love with this young man—but young love can cause so much pain. Martha and Seth needed to talk—that was impossible for now. After Emily left, Seth walked to the hideaway and sat on the stonewall crossing the dam where he and Martha always sat. It was where they shared their dreams, but now it was just a deserted place where he pondered his loneliness. He started up the path to Mexico Road, half way he turned to look once more at that big tree hovering over the blanket of thick grass, its many branches reaching for the clouds—then he closed out a chapter of his life.

Chapter 13

He hoped his father could help him through this difficult time for any lovelorn teenage boy. He found Will sitting in the dining room one rainy day, for Seth it was another day full of melancholy. Seth began to talk, putting aside any thoughts his father might not want to be bothered. He explained how he had fallen prey to a beautiful girl—letting himself believe that she'd be with him when he took over the inn. He learned from her how to be strong willed—now he'd use that quality to drive her from his mind, remove her from his life plan. He decided to make every effort to be a good student, and help his father get well.

Will turned and looked at him with that all-too-familiar blank stare restating his disinterest. Seth had often noticed him sitting in the barroom or dining room, sometimes outside at one of the picnic tables in the grove, staring into space, chain-smoking cigarettes, occasionally sipping on a cup of coffee. However, things were changing for Seth, he wanted the goings-on around him to move ahead in step with his life, he was frustrated and impatient. "You know, you're gonna hafta get off that shit you're taking every day, it's not helping you— it's just making you into a zombie, making you feel and look like hell!" Will lit up another cigarette, ignoring his son's raised voice. "What do you want to know about girls? What makes you think I can help you? I've only been with one woman—your mother." Seth wasn't interested in testing the validity of that claim. He answered, "Because you're older, you're supposed to share the things you've seen in life with me, your son. Guys screw up when they're in love, tell me what the cool guys are supposed to do."

Will's thought processes actually seemed to be working better that particular day. "Let me tell you some things about women for your own good. First, don't act around women like the dumb sons of bitches that come in here. I don't mean the ones that go upstairs, I mean the ones that come here and fart, get drunk, and then go home and scream and slap around their wives and kids." Realizing Will was only half joking, Seth wanted to laugh but he held it back—he had waited for a smile on Will's face, but it didn't come. "Secondly, make sure you keep looking until you're sure you have the right one, because if you get hooked up with the wrong one, one that turns out to be a constant complainer, or lazy, or puts her relatives before her marriage, you're in for a life without one moment of peace."

"How's a guy to know when he's found the right one?" Will was loosening up—gaining confidence—giving fatherly advice—he never gave any before. "There's no foolproof system, the best way is to socialize, meet as many girls as you can until you find one that is pretty in your eyes, nobody else's eyes matter, one that pays you a compliment once in a while, one that squeezes your hand while you're holding it, that kind of stuff."

Seth asked, "What if she's a Brethren girl, and her parents, relatives, her church, everyone she knows, tell her she can't be with a guy because he's an outsider?" Will had heard about Martha—he also knew childhood buddies who went through this same ordeal. "If she loves you, nothing or nobody will keep her away from you." Seth kept listening with mixed feelings. "Is she from that fanatical sect? They're not typical Brethren. Keep telling her you love her, be true to her, don't abuse her—convince her that you want to share your life with her. You'll be able to make her family wrong, and she'll respond to that."

Seth's next question was probably the most important to him. "How could she be in love with me and go away as a missionary without even asking me first?" Will knew his son needed to slow down, no matter how difficult it typically was for a kid his age. "Remember, she isn't old enough to break away. Let her go on her mission, she's probably being pressured to go—she's only seventeen years old. As long as she's living under her family's roof, she's gonna have to do what they say." Will felt the need for a warning. "Just make sure she knows you support her no matter what. If she doubts you'll be there when its time for her to be with you, I guarantee you she'll give you up."

A few days later Seth was helping Katie pick green apples from the old, sturdy apple trees that stood in the inn's picnic grove. They provided the delicious filling for her famous tarts, dumplings and pies served in the dining room. "Grandma, I've been having some good talks with my dad." She was happy hearing that news. "I've been saying to everybody all along, Will Hartman can work out all his problems if people keep him involved!" Her outstretched arms always signaled Seth to step into one of her maternal hugs, embraces that she and Henrietta always used to nourish him over the years while he grew up motherless. "He loves you very much, I know it must have been very hard for you to break through, but keep asking him for advice, ask him to help you—that's what's gonna help him!"

Seth wanted his classmates to know his father was a war hero—a lieutenant colonel in the army, a graduate of West Point. Despite Will's war record, parents kept telling their kids that Will Hartman was crazy, belonged in the "nuthouse," and has to go see a "shrink" just to keep from committing suicide. Now Seth ignored the occasional remark—he had gotten into some fights years earlier with schoolmates who repeated what they heard at home. More importantly, he was older now and didn't feel the need or desire to defend his father's honor with his fists. Besides, he knew Will was getting a little better each month—each year. He was smiling more and began stopping his son as he hurried through the dining room on his way somewhere. Seth took the time to talk—no matter how rushed he was—hoping it'd help Will get alright after so many years of suffering. A lot of people sitting in the bus station restaurant in Rossville would shake their heads when they watched Will board the bus to go to his therapy session. A true test of Seth's maturity was his refusal to be ashamed of the man who fought and made sacrifices for his country.

Chapter 14

Having a relationship with his father was new to him—something he'd always yearned for. He'd missed out on a lot of things most other kids get to experience, but despite that, he still valued his earlier years, recalling the smell of the hay in the barns, the wheat and corn swaying in the fields, the smell of chimney smoke in winter, and feeling the warm breeze that provided relief from the heat and humidity of summer.

During the 1960s, electric service was interrupted more frequently when severe summer thunderstorms or winter snowstorms came. He remembered the flickering flames from those kerosene lamps reflecting off the walls and ceiling, his imagination transporting him back into an earlier era when Sunday school and family picnics, held in the inn's picnic grove, were attended by hundreds of people. While he walked along Mexico Road he'd notice the old retired workhorses, once used to pull the plows and wagons, grazing in the rich pastures, now living out their lives without toil, replaced by the farm tractor.

He often overheard men—sitting at the inn's bar—tell stories about the past that painted portraits hung in the galleries of his imagination. These hard workingmen, with the sight and smell of sweat on their brows and saturating their shirts, would come to the inn and enjoy cold beers at the end of the workday. They were men of the earth—farmers, masons, carpenters, and now since the war's end, many began careers at the steel foundry in Rossville. These hard workers, hard drinkers, hard gamblers—hard sinners were being hurled into the second half of the twentieth century, marked by the arrival of pickup trucks and television. On Saturday nights they came to drink and dance, most to have fun, some looking for trouble—to satisfy all their appetites. If their wives or girlfriends couldn't deal with it, they didn't bring them along.

Seth remembered, beginning when he was eleven or twelve years old, sneaking down the stairs late at night when he was supposed to be in bed sleeping, stealing brief glimpses of them drinking glass after glass from their pitchers of beer and feeling the old wooden dance floor heave up and down as the dancers tortured it.

He heard stories of generations before—young, dancing, singing, and playing their musical instruments on Saturday nights, teasing the girls and stealing kisses and going on long buggy rides watching for ghosts in the woods. All this sent his mind back to the early years of his family's history, to an era that was far more recent than the young boy's comprehension of time realized.

It was August 1961—Martha was away for a year now—he was preparing to begin his senior year in high school. In her letters she kept telling him how much she missed him, and that she didn't know when she'd be coming home, it was out of her control. "My tutor told me to be prepared to spend my senior year of high school here. The only relief I have from being away from you is the fact that I'm helping poor people, especially children. It's hard work, but it's satisfying."

Chapter 15

Henrietta naively believed her seventeen-year-old nephew could be spared exposure to the inn's illicit goings-on. When finding out he was sneaking downstairs at night to witness the antics of the inn's customers she ordered him to stop.

His exposure to the prostitutes was unavoidable—they lived and worked in the second floor rooms adjoining his. He watched the girls hang around in the hallway smoking cigarettes and fixing their hair and adjusting their dresses in front of the floor-length mirror mounted on the bathroom door. He was flattered when they'd ask him if he thought they looked pretty wearing a particular dress or hairdo.

They began teasing him about which girl he wanted to propel him into manhood when he reached the magic age of eighteen. The good-natured razzing continued despite Henrietta warning any who were tempted to take her nephew down the road to sin would regret the indulgence for the rest of their life.

The second floor had the locker-room odor of sweat permeating the stuffy air, carpet smelling of sour beer spilled on it, over and over, one small splash at a time, and the stink of stale cigar and cigarette smoke, long lingering along the ceiling, settling like a seashore smog down on the overstuffed furniture and even the clothing in the closets, coloring everything nicotine yellow. The air instantly changed when a prostitute, drenched in cheap perfume and dusted from head to foot with body powder, walked by inflicting an overwhelming floral scent.

The rooms were like a theatrical set, dingy and dirty in reality, but when lit up for a production, and observed only briefly, they took a new, clean, and bright appearance. Because the prostitutes did their sex production style—each john was there only briefly, the worn paths on the carpet, the frayed sheets, the tattered curtains, the litter kicked under the beds, other imperfections, went unnoticed.

There were seldom more than three prostitutes staying at the inn at any one time. New ones came and went—there was a circuit run by the mob that kept them moving around to save the johns from boredom, but also to prevent the girls from getting too close to their clients—a john falling in love with one of these girls, and a wife making a fuss about it to the cops, could force a raid and arrests.

The girls were never allowed to bring men upstairs by way of the inside stairs—that'd arouse the suspicions of the diners and bar patrons who weren't aware of the upstairs operation.

The girls used the outside stairs that led to the door at the end of the hallway. Eva, a big women who didn't back down from anybody, greeted them there and collected the money. The john then got to perform sex with one of the girls until Eva decided time was up, usually after ten minutes. Rich businessmen, cops, influential politicians, or a friend or business associate of Sal or Ganttrano got to stay longer.

Ganttrano often gave Jonas free time with a girl because of all the drugs he was buying, or to show appreciation for getting him a new drug buyer, usually someone Jonas met at his gun booth. Jonas became a regular client, even when he had to pay.

He was hated and feared by the girls because he manhandled them and demanded rough sex. When he was drunk he got worse. The only consolation was many times he only lasted about a minute or two then passed out, giving the girl the opportunity to escape from the bed without getting beaten.

One cold night he showed up drunk and in an especially abusive mood. After a few minutes of sex with a girl that he had been with before, he barked, "Get dressed, I'm taking you home with me." She nervously told him, "I'm not allowed to go home with a customer." He gave her a drunken stare while swaying back and forth, then grabbed her, punched her in the face, and threw her across the room. Pausing to catch his breath—he ripped open the door and started dragging her, still nude, by the hair down the hall toward the door to the outside steps. She was screaming and kicking, violently swinging her arms when he lifted her up and put her over his shoulder. Eva came out of her room just as he got to the end of the hall. "Put the girl down now, I'm not taking any shit from you!" Reaching for the door, he swung around and grabbed Eva by the throat and pushed her with his free arm as far as he could—she weighed three hundred pounds, so she didn't move that far. Staggering back and regaining her balance by grabbing onto the door jam, she reached inside her room for her baseball bat, and just like Katie did years earlier in the barroom, she started swinging it, getting the back of his legs just as he stepped outside onto the small landing at the top of the stairs. Crying out from the pain, he fell back inside the hallway, landing on top of the girl. While she frantically struggled to get out from under him, Eva whacked him across the chest. When he got to his feet, holding his arms over his face in defense, she whacked him across his left arm. You could hear it break—he moaned in agony and fell through the door ripping it off its hinges. Back onto the landing, he tried to navigate down the stairs without missing any steps, but missed plenty, falling down most of the way, bouncing off the railing on each side like the chrome ball in a pinball machine. Ganttrano heard the commotion and came running out of the bar to find Jonas lying on the ground. Eva yelled down to him. "You keep that fuckin son of a bitch out of this place or I'm gonna tell Sal that the prick comes here and beats my whores, someday he's gonna really hurt somebody." Ganttrano didn't like being threatened, but he realized Eva meant what she said, and that Sal would listen to her.

Later that night Ganttrano came upstairs and beat the girl Jonas had wanted to take home. Hearing the girl's screams, Eva came running into the room protesting. He said, "Every time you threaten me, I'm gonna come up here and beat one of your girls, and I'm gonna beat her until she's black and blue bad enough she can't work for a fuckin week." He didn't scare her—she tried to talk sense to him. "That ain't gonna solve the problem we're having with Jonas Konrad. You're just putting a girl out of work, costing her money, me money, and Sal money, and if he finds out, he's gonna be pissed off." Bill shot back, "I'll keep Konrad under control, you just make sure he gets what he comes here for, and don't give me or him any shit about it."

On nights when Big John ran his card game, held in the back room of the cellar, the girls didn't make any appointments. Players were charged a cover charge—Sal got that, and Big John got to keep the "house" cut of every pot bet. About forty-five to fifty men attended these gambling sessions—not all at one time—usually eight to ten played any one particular night. The girls walked along the path from the outside stairs to the back of the inn and down the old rickety wooden stairs into the cellar to serve the drinks and food, and during breaks or after the game broke up, were available to the players for sex upstairs or, for less money, on the parking lot in their cars.

Seth would lie awake and listen from his open bedroom window as the girls struggled to walk in the dark in their high heels without tripping and falling, and then later leading their customers back up the path to the stairs. Trying to overhear their conversations wasn't easy because of the loud jukebox playing country songs about betrayed love seeping out the barroom windows. He dozed off to the smell of French fries being deep-fried, blown out into the night air and up into his window by the gigantic kitchen exhaust fan.

Chapter 16

There was a curtain drawn across the second-floor hallway—it separated the rooms at the far end where the girls lived and conducted their business from the rooms where Seth and the other family members lived. Eva had two rooms, one where she stayed while greeting the johns and supervising the girls, the other across from Seth's where she lived with her young daughter Joanne, who just returned to live with her after staying for two years with her aunt, Eva's sister, in Pittsburgh. Ganttrano lived in one of the inn's two apartments on the first floor—Big John lived in the other.

Joanne, a year older than Seth, had long natural red hair and thousands of freckles, she was very statuesque—was built like a model—attractive but not a beauty. When living with Eva earlier, before Eva came to the Oregon Inn, she had begun at an early age engaging in sex and using alcohol and drugs. When she graduated from high school the previous spring, her aunt phoned Eva to tell her Joanne was being sent back to her, she had enough of the stress endured while raising her. Eva made arrangements with Ganttrano for the girl to work with Katie in the kitchen.

Joanne was at the inn for a few days when she noticed Seth and used her smile and experience to draw him into conversation. They began meeting at first on the second-floor porch, or they'd eat at the same table in the dining room. She told him, "I'm not gonna make the same mistakes my mother made, having sex with cheap johns until I'm some old bitch with no money and no future." She told Seth that in her young days Eva was a slender high priced call girl in New York. "Now, forty years later, she's babysitting these temperamental young sluts, making sure they don't rip off the johns, keeping the johns from beating the hell out of 'em, and guaranteeing the cops, politicians, and big spenders the best service money, power and influence can get—it makes me sick to my stomach." Adding to Eva's problems was Ganttrano beating the girls after closing time if a john complained about being slighted in any way.

When Henrietta noticed Joanne spending time with Seth she figured he was developing a romantic interest in her, which she mistakenly believed would be good for him, helping him get over Martha. She should have realized that the daughter of a whorehouse madam wouldn't be a good influence for her young inexperienced nephew. Instead, because she was now in denial—pretending the racketeering her criminal husband had established at the inn was just harmless naughtiness—she naïvely believed that Seth and Joanne could have a normal teenage romance, limited to kissing and handholding—"going steady". She mentioned to Eva that perhaps she could encourage Joanne to go out with him. "He's never had a normal girlfriend, one he can take to the movies, or for ice cream, go bowling with—do things with other high school couples." She added, "This Brethren girl he's in love with isn't allowed to be with him, now she went away for a year or two, and the girls from high school only want him to parade around like a trophy—their 'Prince Charming'." Eva told her she'd talk with Joanne.

Joanne was filing and polishing her fingernails when Eva described her concept of teenage romance—Joanne had heard it before—it wasn't the same as Henrietta's. "Henrietta wants you to take Seth to bed. He's a virgin, so be patient and take him slowly, make sure you tell him he can fuck you as long as he wants—maybe then he won't be so anxious." She was giving instructions to her daughter like a factory foreman would lead a worker through a production order. "While he's fucking you, convince him no man has ever made you feel that good, moan a little, and make sure you don't tell him that it was his aunt's idea—do you understand?" Joanne looked up and answered with a trace of sarcasm, "Of course I understand mother, don't I always do what you say?"

Seth had begun turning the lights off at his end of the hallway, then crawling out on the floor and peeking around the edge of the curtain, watching the steady parade of johns coming upstairs.

Occasionally he got an opportunity to peek in the keyhole or the crack in the door of one of the rooms while a girl was servicing a customer. On one occasion Kelly, one of the prettiest girls, walked out of the room to use the bathroom just as he was kneeling down to look. She never hesitated. After returning from the bathroom, she said, "Make sure you keep quiet if you wanna watch." She left the door open about two inches, giving him a panoramic view—he got a graphic lesson in sexual technique. He always had the chance to see a lot during the day when the girls weren't working, doing their laundry, bathing, fixing their nails and hair—they were so accustomed to him being there they walked or sat about with little or no clothing on.

One night while he was peeking through the curtain, Joanne slid up alongside of him, startling him. "Shhh, keep quiet, my mother will be really pissed off if she finds out we're spying like this, we could scare off one of these pricks if any notice us." They felt safe—they wouldn't be caught as long as Henrietta, Katie, or Will didn't come up the stairs from the dining room.

She got closer and whispered into his ear, "If I kiss you, do you wanna kiss me back?" Seth didn't want to appear too anxious, but it was difficult to harness the excitement—he hadn't kissed a girl for a long time. He smiled. His heart was racing. She leaned over, and they kissed on the lips and then opened their mouths, their tongues meeting while he slid on top of her.

After they made out for a while she asked, "Do you smoke?" Before he could answer, she whispered, "I drink whiskey, and I got some weed. Meet me out back later." Soon, on most nights, they'd sneak down stairs after the inn closed and Seth would steal more cigarettes and Joanne would pour some shots into a paper cup from each bottle of opened bourbon and take it up to his room and mix it with a can or two of ginger ale. With him and Martha, they'd drink beer and the first whiskey he happened to grab. Joanne was more sophisticated, she preferred good bourbon. Sometimes she'd put some into an old cough syrup bottle and hide it under her bed. Seth got himself a cough syrup bottle so he could take the bourbon to his best friend Lester Noll and the girls they started inviting to the an abandoned cabin at the far end of the Noll farm, once used by itinerant farm workers. The cabin hadn't been used for years and had cracked windows, a leaky roof, and rusted off door hinges—to close it and keep animals out, it had to be laid against the jam and propped shut with a large, thick tree limb. Inside was an old metal bed frame with a straw mattress, and a small wooden table and a chair.

Marijuana couldn't be stolen because Ganttrano controlled all the drugs. Joanne would ask each of the prostitutes for a joint or two and then give Seth all he needed for his and Lester's cabin parties.

After their next long kiss a few days later, she allowed herself to get aroused—easy for her—he was a very handsome guy, and she knew she had the go ahead to take him all the way. They went to his room, got undressed and began kissing passionately. When he got inside her she wrapped her arms and legs around him tightly responding to his slow and smooth rhythm, increasing to a feverish pace as they finished together. He lay there next to her, the smell of her all over him, and closed his eyes to relive in his mind all the details of the last hour. Finally he turned to her and said, "I didn't use a rubber, what are we going to do if I get you pregnant?" Joanne, thinking that could possibly be a good thing, answered him truthfully. "You don't have to worry, I'm on the pill, but don't you think you should have thought about a rubber before we screwed?" Seth felt she should share some of the irresponsibility; she came on to him fast, if she would've gone slower he could've easily gotten a condom—there were plenty on the inn's second floor. He was making excuses—anyhow he didn't want to think about that right now. "I think you and I could become comfortable being lovers." Joanne asked, "What does that mean, comfortable being lovers?" He didn't answer—they both went to sleep.

When the morning sun glaring in the window awoke her, she slipped out of his room and into hers—already regretting being sucked into yet another romance to keep secret—she had more than her share of those, beginning when she was a little girl—wise to the fact that her and Seth having sex wasn't what Henrietta had in mind for them despite what her mother said. It was always hard for her to resist believing her mother's lies—sex isn't complicated at all, give men what they want and the woman gets what she wants. In reality, Joanne had a kid still in high school wanting her to move across the hall into his room because she has the experience to give him what he wants. For her it was one sided, just giving, not taking, becoming a victim because she had no idea what she wanted, knowing she was doomed if she soon didn't find out.

On the other hand, Seth knew exactly what he wanted— the Oregon Inn, and knowing that he was going to eventually get it freed him from stress when it came to girls. He didn't need Joanne, despite what she believed, to bolster his ego with sex, and he had no worries at school about dating because

Laura Sheridan, the most beautiful girl at school, was his girlfriend. He knew Joanne and Laura were both made possible because of the inn—Joanne because of the inn's corruption—Laura was with him because of the gossip about it. Careful not to become too cynical, he decided to harvest the benefits regardless of their reasons, or for that matter, any other women and their motives

Six months earlier, near the end of his junior year, he had made out with Laura, and soon they were doing a lot of it, mostly at school dances, on the school bus, or walking back Mexico Road from the bus stop. Laura was sophisticated, well built with short brown hair, brown eyes and a pretty face that most artists would want to paint. Her wardrobe was the envy of all the other girls—she usually wore big, bulky knit turtleneck sweaters, short, short skirts, and oxblood penny loafers, all bought at the best stores. She was always dressed like the older college girls that went to the best girls' schools. For special occasions she liked to wear dresses with spaghetti straps, dangling earrings, and a thin chain around her neck.

Setting aside fears of rejection and ignoring the social correctness of the 1960s, Laura came to Seth and told him she wanted to be his girlfriend. She heard he was a wild hell brand that drank, smoked cigarettes, used marijuana and supplied the contraband for Lester's parties. She could have any boy, they all wanted her, but she wanted him because his reputation excited her—his family was in organized crime. Even though Laura would never think of going to any of Lester's parties, she wanted a boyfriend who was not only a bad boy, she wanted "the bad boy".

Many times privileged girls are snobs, but Laura wasn't—she'd say hello and talk to everyone, never talking bad about anyone, the other school girls adored her and looked up to her. Her father was very wealthy, an engineer who, along with two other wealthy industrialists, owned their own specialty steel company. Laura's mother was a trained ballerina—she had danced in New York and Paris, now she gave private lessons, and was a housewife. Laura's younger brother was eight years old.

She had faults, but they made her even more irresistible. She was absentminded. She squinted because she never could get accustomed to wearing her eyeglasses. Mornings she'd unroll the plastic rollers in her hair but miss combing out some of the curls, coming to school with one or two just dangling—girls competing to hurriedly comb out her hair in the bathroom before classes began. She was always running fifteen to thirty minutes behind schedule. Having Laura as his girlfriend was a status symbol, but Seth knew falling in love with her would cause him a lot of misery. Martha's family had objected to him because he was from outside their church—he had expected that from the beginning of their relationship, and he had to accept it, but he wasn't about to put himself through that kind of frustration again—Laura's parents would never allow her to marry a man who wasn't from a wealthy family and well placed in society.

Seth agreed to go steady with her—that fall they became seniors, and the younger kids all looked up to the storybook couple. Their relationship was, in truth, a myth, she was happy because she had Seth, tall and handsome with his classic good looks and black hair, to show off, but all she'd ever give in return was bragging rights—he got to smell her perfume, hold her hand, and make out with her—he got to take her to school dances, football games, and birthday parties.

When Seth and Laura made out she never allowed it to go beyond kissing. She had learned very young her family's rules—remain a virgin until she found a man that met muster with her parents, probably some Ivy League college kid, maybe a football player, somebody that wasn't from where Seth Hartman was from.

Ironically, Seth really was wealthy, but nobody ever thought about it, not even him. The Oregon Inn, including its twenty-five acres of pristine woodland and its equipment and liquor license, even though it had a market value of half of what it should've been because of the racketeering, had substantial value. Seth knew someday it'd be worth a lot more. However, to Laura's parents, and Martha's before, it was a cesspool of corruption run by a disreputable crime family.

Lester Noll was a farm boy and high school football player, short, good-looking, but not handsome, a bow legged rough neck, who was outgoing, sincere, very charming with a good sense of humor, but also a braggart. Because of his legs he walked with an awkward swagger, but there wasn't any hint of it when he played fast and forceful on the football field. His short brown hair was almost always disheveled and he chewed tobacco when working on the farm, mostly to mimic his father. He made sure to brush his teeth every morning—he knew girls didn't like brownish, yellowish tobacco teeth.

October arrived with the crisp chilly nights of harvest season. Seth and Lester decided to go on a Halloween hayride with the local church youth group, but Seth needed a date because Laura wasn't allowed to go on hayrides. Lester fixed him up with a girl name Mandy from Eisentown, the next town over from Alton Manor, about ten miles away. Lester asked, "You remember her don't you? Last year, when we played football against her school, she was the cute little brunette cheerleader who came running over to us after the game and congratulated us for the win. She got hell from her fellow cheerleaders for doing that, but she couldn't resist—she had the "hots" for me." Seth didn't remember her. "You didn't do it with her did you? I'm not going out with her if you did." Lester said, "No, I didn't bang her, I could have, she kept calling me for weeks, but man, I can't have 'em all!" Lester relished his role as Seth's mentor when it came to girls, and was happy his friend wasn't a virgin anymore thanks to Joanne. "You can have a good time with Mandy, she's experienced, the kind of chick you need right now—so don't be shy!"

A few weeks earlier, when Seth had told him he had sex with Joanne, he reacted predictably. "Congratulations shit head! Its about time you got laid, I was beginning to wonder—I knew you weren't gonna get any pussy from Martha." Seth didn't mind any of his best friend's teasing except when he mentioned Martha. "Don't talk about her like that. She wanted us to wait, so I said we'd wait. If I would have insisted she would've done it with me because she loves me—at least she did then."

Lester didn't want to hear anymore about Martha. "I hope this Joanne chick helps you get over Martha. She's not good for you Seth—it was always disgusting when you were with her. She made you lovesick, we never had any fun because she always ruled you, never wanting you to be cool or letting you just hang out."

The noisy farm tractor, pulling and jerking the wagon along the country lane on that dark and chilly night, gave the teenage couples opportunity to hug and kiss and be in love, a chance to cuddle under the thick blankets on the bed of straw. Seth, noticing Lester and his date Linda Jennings getting carried away—he was on top of her, the blanket moving up and down, felt forced to keep a vigil, distracting the minister and his wife if they began to turn and notice, despite the darkness, what Lester and Linda were doing. Seth's evening got even worse when Mandy became angry with him for being distracted and not making out with her. Lester got very lucky that night— Seth didn't get lucky at all.

After the hayride ended, while everyone else was having punch and cookies in the church hall, Seth took Lester aside. "I ought to kick your ass for pulling a stunt like that. A church hayride with the minister and his wife in the front of the wagon isn't the time or the place for screwing a girl." Lester reached out to put Seth in a headlock—and while Seth resisted they stumbled over each other's feet, and then embraced in a bear hug—it's what they always did after squabbling.

They had become best friends in fifth grade, mostly because they were never rivals. Not what you'd call handsome, Lester attracted girls because he could charm them, and they overlooked him being loud and boisterous because he was the star quarterback on the high school football team and a county sports all-star.

Seth attracted girls because he was handsome, and he was quiet and gentle, which many interpreted as being mysterious. Seth also played football, but just enough to get by. For most of the girls, not just Laura, the thought of being with him was exciting because he was a member of an organized crime family.

Lester found that very amusing. "I wonder what the fathers of the those little princesses would do if they knew their daughters were offering you pussy just because your uncle is a goddamn gangster!"

The first time Seth had sex at Lester's cabin it was with Doris Foss, a cute, slender, natural blond. Doris and her buxom friend Kay Clark were city girls from Rossville who often visited Kay's grandparents who lived next to the Noll farm. Lester had met them a few times while they were taking a walk along Mexico Road. He'd walk along, using his charm to flatter them and making them laugh with his jokes. He told them about his best friend Seth, and then arranged for the four of them to rendezvous at the cabin.

Doris, two years older than Seth, attended Rossville Secretarial School and had a boyfriend who was in the air force—she was lonely.

Their tongues met the instant they were alone and he began touching her everywhere, her stored up passion causing her arms and hands to move all over him as she pulled him to her. The stale air in the cabin let on the harsh fragrance of the lacquer spray in her stiff teased-up hair. He smelled her mellow sensuous perfume and tasted her makeup and lipstick while kissing her face and neck, before moving to her breasts. Making love to her wasn't like making love to Joanne. Joanne always took control—teaching with patience, using techniques developed from experience. With Doris, a girl he hardly knew, which only increased his excitement, he was in control and had to keep in check his youthful yearning, trying to stay calm, wanting to prolong the sex, satisfying his desire secondary to bolstering his ego, he wanted to do better than her boyfriend, satisfying her and getting encores. He had begun helping himself to condoms kept in the prostitute's night tables, ensuring that he and Lester would always have an ample supply. He slowly entered her but finished almost immediately—she sighed and smiled, a look of contentment on her face. He realized her expectations were aligned with his limited experience and performance. It would've been a disappointment for Joanne, but it was very fulfilling for Doris.

Later they lay in the grass in back of the cabin and talked while Lester and Kay were inside. Seth said, "I think I'd like to live in the city, there's got to be so much to do." Doris described the life of a teenager in Rossville. "There's always dances somewhere, movie theaters, we go bowling a lot. You need to come in town and spend the day with me." He smiled at the thought of all the excitement and freedom. "I'd like that, I got my driver's license now, but I don't have a car. I have to depend on my aunt letting me use the inn's station wagon—not very cool!" They both laughed, she said "I think that as long as a car has four wheels and a motor to make 'em go around, who cares if it's cool or not?" He was glad to hear a girl with that attitude. He got serious. "What about your boyfriend, when's he coming home?" She hedged, not wanting to talk about that. "He'll be home for two weeks next month—he wrote and told me he wants to get engaged while he's on leave." The following week Seth did drive into Rossville and met Doris at the bowling alley. They sat in the snack bar and talked. "Seth, I'd like to go with you, but I'd never be able to choose between you and him. I'm not sorry we did it, and I hope you're not." Seth was relieved, he never intended to ask her to go with him—seeing her again made him realize he wasn't attracted to her. Going to see her when he had a girl like Martha in love with him made him feel like a fool. He really was, but he was still feeling sorry for himself, punishing Martha for leaving him.

He kept smuggling the bourbon, cigarettes, and marijuana out of the inn with Joanne's help, telling her only guys came to the cabin parties—she didn't believe that lie, but she had to accept it—she wanted and needed a man. Despite her sophistication, she let herself get hooked on him, convinced she'd never find another one with his gentleness, honesty, and youthful innocence. She was sleeping with him almost every night now, and nobody was noticing except Eva, who gave her some motherly advice, "Don't fall in love with the kid, you'll get so fucked up in the head you'll be unbearable to live with." Joanne kept her mouth shut—remembering the quickest way to get her mother's shut was to agree with her. Eva went on, "I know all the tricks, all the bullshit, so if you're thinking about stopping the pill and getting knocked up so he marries you, think again, because they'll never let him marry you, not in a million fuckin years." Joanne had enough and stormed out of the room without saying a word. Eva didn't let up, yelling down the hall before Joanne could go outside, slamming the door, "You'll just cause everybody around here grief, and I won't help you get out of any goddamn mess you get your ass into, remember that!"

When Kay showed up at the cabin with another girl, she told Seth that Doris' boyfriend had come home. "She's spending all her time with him. I think they're gonna get engaged, she told me she's gonna stop cheating on him."

Jeannie Canton was a tall girl with slender cone-shaped breasts, short brown hair, and a pretty face with full voluptuous lips and long gorgeous legs. She usually wore, almost like a uniform, denim short shorts—short-sleeved pullover knit shirts, small gold earrings in her pierced ears and opened-toed flip-flop sandals. She had played sports in high school and now was in her freshman year at the state teachers college about sixty-five miles away—she lived on campus and came home weekends—her career goal was to be a gym teacher and girl's basketball coach.

Seth was quickly attracted to her, but soon found out having sex with her was like working out—with Jeannie he learned the difference between having sex and making love. At least he and Joanne cared for each other—it wasn't love, but they liked each other. With Doris it was passion, she was hungry to be loved, and he had wanted to give her pleasure. He told Lester, "With Jeannie it's all physical, getting relieved—coming—getting off." Having sex with Jeannie wasn't satisfying for him, and at the same time the guilt of betraying Martha was beginning to bother him. He had sex with Jeannie one time—it was on the day he met her. He never saw her again.

Walking home from school, he told Lester how he felt. "I miss Martha, girls like Jeannie are just interested in sex. I want more than that when I make love to a girl." Lester stopped walking, and Seth took a few more steps, stopped and turned around, prepared for Lester's rant. "Let me get this straight, you're unfulfilled with a beautiful girl like Jeannie because she's only interested in your cock!" He paused as if waiting for Seth's nod. "Most guys think that's like dying and going to heaven, you dumb ass. If somebody asked Kay to describe in detail my face or my cock, perhaps she'd do better—." Seth stopped him, "Don't give me any shit, you know what I'm talking about—be serious. Maybe Kay is the type of girl you want—or need, but it's not what I'm looking for—give me a break!" They started walking again, Lester adding, "I'm sorry, I just don't want to see Martha get you all messed up again. Kay and I do get into some heavy sex, but we're starting to have some feelings for each other—she's talking about spending the summer with her grandparents. If she does I figure I'll be a daddy before long—walking down the aisle, saying I do, all that shit that goes with living your life." Seth was surprised to hear his best friend talk so earnestly. "Lester, those things are OK as long as that's what you want. Your family has a farm that's worth a lot of money, and you're an only child like me. So maybe we'll both get chances a lot of guys don't get, but if you want to be a doctor, a teacher, or maybe a lawyer, you can't be knocking up a girl the summer after graduating from high school." He wanted to be supportive of his best friend—he was sorry what he said about Kay. She was perky, almost "bimbolike", wore her light brown hair short and curly, she had big breasts and an outgoing personality. What many people failed to realize when first meeting her was how smart she was—a straight-A student in high school, well read, with a developing mind for business and crunching numbers.

Joanne, sitting with Seth on the inn's porch, asked, "What did you mean that day, after we did it the first time, when you said we were comfortable being lovers?" He told her he wasn't sure what he meant, he barely remembered saying it. She said, "I think it means you get to screw me because I happen to live right here, and you can still have your girlfriends and pals to party with." He was surprised by her frankness—he knew he was using her, but he believed she was a user too.

Eva feared her daughter might cause problems, convinced she got spoiled sleeping with Seth. Joanne no longer felt grateful that she didn't have to begin a life of selling herself to a stranger who might be forty years older than her, maybe a drunk, a junkie, or violent, diseased, hopelessly poor or rich and greedy. Now she was ready to tell Seth that she wanted a man who could offer her more, one who was interested in making a life with her, not just wanting her because she was always available.

They came to the same conclusion at the same time—they needed to end their relationship. She wanted to be in love, get married, have children, and not be known as the daughter of a whorehouse madam. He understood now that youthful lust was the superficial reason he had sex with Joanne, and also Doris and Jeanne. The primary reason was selfishness—he was willing to betray Martha and make a mockery of their love to punish her for abandoning him. Perhaps, to be fair to himself, the reason for much of his transgression was being hurt so badly that there was a chance even some neurosis was present—he had a truly exceptional love for her, feelings for her that he was forced to hide to protect her from her family. Now he was wise enough to know time was running out for them, he had to clean up his behavior, he had to wait for her to come home, and then they both had to settle the issues that had always threatened their relationship.

A few days later Joanne broke some more bad news to him. "Ganttrano wants me to start turning tricks, one of the girls told him she over heard my mother and me arguing, and he made her tell him everything." Seth saw the signs of fear on her face, he heard it in her voice, and watched her tremble while he helped her light a cigarette. "She can't say no to him because Sal wants a young local girl he can periodically send to entertain his best friends in Rossville. Bill told my mom that he's gonna screw me before I start working—she's gonna have to do what he says to keep peace." Seth was furious—he knew Joanne was a victim before she came to the Oregon Inn, now to see her become a victim while here, especially if the sex she had with him added to her anguish, bothered him. He was pacing back and forth, determined to stop the disgusting plan. "Don't do it, don't let Ganttrano get what he wants, you don't need to do what he says, you're not a whore. I'll talk to Aunt Henrietta and she'll talk to Uncle Sal—I'll put a stop to this."

He was walking in circles now—she stood up and stopped him, putting her fingertips gently on his lips. "Please don't say anything, that'll just make him go crazy—he'll make my mother's life a more living hell than it already is." He looked into her eyes, and for the first time he noticed there was some innocence and vulnerability, how could he have missed seeing it when he made love to her? "I hope you can forgive me for not treating you better, when we were in bed it was such great sex, I'd fantasize about totally climbing inside you, I mean my whole self! I did have feelings for you. I hope you believe that. I think you deserve to find happiness, and I hope you find it."

She needed to hear him say that. She said, "You don't have to apologize for us having sex, you didn't hold a gun to my head, I enjoyed it as much as you did. Its just time for me to get the hell out of here and find something more." She gave him a gentle kiss on the lips and then, before leaving his room, whispered in his ear—"Sometimes I think you got maybe half your whole self in me anyway."

Eva had run away from home when she was fourteen-years old, and over the years had only contacted her mother sporadically when she was in desperate need of help. She had helped raise Joanne, rescuing and sheltering her granddaughter whenever Eva got thrown in jail or took up with a man who was a bigger than usual loser or abuser. Eva had promised her, when Joanne was a little girl, she wouldn't allow her to become a prostitute, and knowing her daughter was now standing at a life's crossroads, she found herself forced to keep her promise— she called her mother and asked for help once more. It was time to fess up to the facts—girls that grow up and live with prostitutes, more than likely become one.

On a cold morning, about 3:30 AM, the inn was dark and quiet except for the clanging hot water pipes and a radio's muffled love ballads coming from somebody's room, Eva packed Joanne an extra set of clothing and some essentials and woke her without warning, telling her to get dressed and keep very quiet. Outside was a taxi waiting to take her to the bus station, then off to secretarial school. "Your grandmother will be waiting for you at the bus depot in Pittsburgh." They hugged, but there weren't any tears, or even goodbyes.

Seth woke up that morning and found a hastily written note on his end table. She confessed Henrietta and Eva urged her to become his friend. "They wanted us together, but I don't believe the sex was your aunt's idea, she just wanted you to have a girl to go out with so you'd get over your girlfriend—she don't like her. I'm pretty sure the sex part was only my mother's idea—another way for her to create more entanglements that she has always believed further her job security." She apologized for going along with the ruse, pleading with him to remember that his aunt had the best intentions—wanting him to be happy. "After it began as a favor to them, I started caring for you, I'm not sorry for anything we did, and I hope you're not. I know I was the first girl you went all the way with, so I guess you'll never forget me because of that. I know I'll never forget you, you made me very happy, Love, Joanne."

During the previous weeks, Seth had begun to make progress dealing with his failings and the guilt they generated, but her note caused him some inner conflict mostly because she hadn't spoke to him like she wrote to him. He was relieved she didn't, at the start of their love affair he was so inexperienced and vulnerable he surely would've fallen in love with her, then would've hurt her and put himself in the middle of a big mess when Martha came home. At times, to justify using her, he had thought of her as just another prostitute. Then again there were times when he felt he wanted to be her friend, he believed she'd be a good and loyal one, and he longed for a girl he could talk to like he always could with Martha. Now that Joanne was gone he knew all that remained was living the big sham in his life, being Laura Sheridan's boyfriend. He never feared falling in love with her because the only purpose of their relationship, which had remained harmless because it was conceived as such, was to escort her out of high school and off to college into the waiting arms and dorm bed of some future doctor or lawyer.

Chapter 17

After turning eighteen years old and graduating from high school, Seth decided to take the summer of 1962 off before finally pursuing his birthright—the Hartman next in line to run the Oregon Inn. He was ready to learn how to do it, and then oversee its renewal and revitalization despite the current bad goings-on that made it appear hopeless. Everyone, including Sal, thought Will was the owner of the inn, but Katie was the sole stockholder of the corporation that owned it—she had wisely held off over the years signing the stock over to Will because of his mental state. She had Seth drive her to Jacob Weaver's office—he was the family lawyer, so he could explain the details of the inn's ownership to him. "Seth, the inn's affairs are confidential. Your grandmother, your father, me, and now you, are the only people that know the details of the ownership." He knew that his father, while drunk or high on drugs, would've given the inn away years ago if he would've had the legal right to do so. "We don't want to publicize the details of ownership because of the problems that currently exist on the property, so you need to make sure you don't discuss it with anyone." Seth nodded—he could appreciate what Weaver was saying, and he decided then and there to listen to the advice of people who are paid to protect the interests of the family. Weaver said, "Your grandmother is anxious to transfer ownership to you and your father, as soon as one or both of you are able to take over."

On the way back to the inn Katie took Seth to one of the Rossville car dealerships and bought him a used pick-up truck. She couldn't have bought him a better gift.

Many of his classmates were going on to college, joining the military, working the family farm, and some, like Lester, decided they wanted to learn how to build houses. An exclusive girls' school in New England had accepted Laura. She never called him—she left the month after graduation to spend August in Europe before starting class.

She had walked over to him after the graduation ceremony and kissed him on the cheek. "I'll never forget you," she said, then turned and walked away with her parents. They were the storybook couple of the senior class, but because it was all a charade—he wasn't surprised when she showed how little he meant to her. He recalled her telling him that she wasn't ever coming back after college to godforsaken Alton Manor. He told her not to be so certain—Mexico Road had always taken back its natives, over the years many had left, became disillusioned and defeated, victims of the hypocrisy and evils of the rest of the world, then fled home to the white gravel road and its extremities, with farms and homesteads securely attached. Perhaps Laura would be different, she had grown up with money, usually getting whatever she asked for, and Seth knew she'd never marry a man without plenty of money to keep her very comfortable.

Henrietta found Seth sitting in a chair pulled up to the edge on the front porch, his chin resting on his arms, folded and lying on top of the porch railing. "You look like your mind is a million miles away, do you miss Laura?" He turned his head and looked up at her, "I don't miss her, why would I miss her? He finally explained to Henrietta the make-believe relationship he had with Laura. "She's a beautiful girl, but she's a phony, status-seeking bitch." He added, "I put up with her because she was a status symbol, a beautiful trophy, and she kept my mind off Martha. But I guess it made me a phony too."

Henrietta didn't want to hear anything about Martha, was tempted to say so, but chose not to confront him. She wished she had discouraged him when he first became attracted to her—convinced Martha would never disappoint her family and marry outside their church. Henrietta was being proven right— the girl left to work in some third world country for a church that'd never accept the young man she supposedly loved.

He appreciated her listening—reminded during his years of growing up she and Katie were the two wise women who always guided and advised him. Henrietta was special to him— a great lady

He never mentioned Joanne—he would probably forgive her eventually for using the girl to meddle in his life.

In the beginning of the year Katie, only sixty-four years old, fell and broke her hip and needed to go into a nursing home to get help with everyday living and for physical therapy to aid her recovery. Reluctantly, and over Seth's objections, she agreed to go live at the Country View Nursing Home in Rossville. He visited her every week.

During these visits they mostly talked about her health and his ambitions. Katie said, "Don't take life so seriously!" She reached out and put her hand under his chin, squeezing it and turning his face so she could look into his eyes, "Let things take their course, Martha grew up being pressured, she'll rebel sooner or later because she's a smart girl who can think for herself." He appreciated her optimism. "When I'm not worried about losing her, I'm worried about harm coming to her." Katie said, "She can take care of herself, just help her whenever you can. You need to quit smoking and drinking, take care of yourself so that when she's finally with you, both of you can live a good long life." She forced him to face the real issue and agree to accept the way things are meant to be. "You gotta realize sooner or later she'll have to choose between her family and you. If she chooses her family, you gotta accept it, and despite the hurt you'll feel you mustn't hate her. The decision will be tough for her, she was raised differently than you—honor her even if she gives you up and chooses to stay Brethren—accept it."

Chapter 18

On July 21, 1962, a hot and sunny day, Ben Kaiser's body was discovered floating in Lorraine Creek with his head blown off by a shotgun blast. The county coroner used the body's fingerprints to make a positive identification and then ruled the death a homicide—this was no hunting accident. Police investigators began recreating a scenario of what they thought probably happened.

They knew that Jonas and Ben went pheasant hunting. Freda had confirmed that while being interviewed by detective Paul Marberg from the U.S. Attorney's office in Philadelphia, who had been spending some time in the neighborhood investigating suspected illegal gun dealing by Jonas. Marberg was a short stocky man with his black wooly hair cut in crew-cut style—he wore the typical justice department dark business suit, spoke slowly and quietly—taking lengthy pauses between questions to write notes in his small notepad that he carried in his shirt's left breast pocket. The information Freda provided allowed him to make an educated guess that the two men had quarreled over gun selling, but after being questioned further, she admitted the two men might have argued over women, in particular about Aryan children being born on the Konrad farm. Jonas, finding out Freda was barren, was intent on finding another woman—possibly Martha Dern, to impregnate.

Marberg figured that if they indeed argued over women, Jonas might have confessed to Ben that he wanted Martha Dern because she was the perfect candidate—Brethren: genetically pure because her German ancestors never married outside the church. She was slender and young—she had a beautiful face, was blue eyed and hopefully very fertile, all traits desirous when bearing children fathered by a handsome, robust German man. Jonas wasn't handsome or robust, and his mind was becoming more deranged as time passed, but he denied all that—convinced their sons would be handsome and strong like him, the daughters beautiful like her. Each child born would be one more step toward the fulfillment of Adolph Hitler's dream of a perfect race.

Jonas had treated Martha badly quite a few times—being harsh mostly to suppress his wanting her, trying hard not to violate a very important rule, permitting infatuation to undermine the pursuit of his twisted goals. He sometimes imagined Martha actually wanting to be the mother of his children, not having to rape her—she'd want him to get her pregnant. Of course, that was never going to happen. It was all fantasy.

Marberg had some questions for Jonas—he had agreed to cooperate. "I went hunting with Kaiser, I decided to come back, and he decided to stay out in the woods. That's the last time I saw him. That's all I have to say." Marberg didn't expect any more. He knew Jonas killed Ben Kaiser, but he couldn't prove it.

Only Jonas and Ben were there, nobody really knew what happened except Jonas, but as time passed the story pieces came together. Jonas killed Ben because he confessed going to Orbachville to threaten and scare Martha, then beating her when things got out of control. Not suspecting Jonas's volatile feelings about the girl, he told him he decided to rape her, but after putting up a lot of resistance, she was rescued by one of her schoolmates. Jonas, shocked when he heard Ben's story, stopped walking and gasped for breath. He reminded him of his orders not to confront her, and quickly concluded Ben's motivation wasn't his fear of what Martha saw, it was his wish to rape her. They began to argue—Ben repeated earlier criticism of Jonas not being a more aggressive leader and not having the girl killed when it was suspected she had peered in the springhouse window. With bulging eyes, Jonas screamed at Ben for trying to rape the girl he secretly wanted himself. The infatuation was poisoning his ability to lead, bringing on emotional outrage so intense he felt as if his brain was boiling.

The arguing continued, suddenly Jonas became calm and quiet—they began walking down the trail until they got to a small stream, pausing to rest before crossing it. Ben felt more at ease now that Jonas had apparently recovered from his outrage. Instead, without any warning, Jonas raised his shotgun and fired both barrels into Ben's head, blowing it clear off. Unruffled, he picked up some large leaves and wiped his face of the speckles of Kaiser's blood that had reached him.

Chapter 19

Her mother wrote her telling about the murder of Ben Kaiser just a mile from their farm, and Martha contacted Emily right away asking to come home because she'd be safe now.

The day after Martha got home she went to visit Katie, she had phoned the inn to talk with her but was told she now resided at Country View. Katie jumped to her feet, clapped her hands, and reached out for the young girl. "You look so pretty! How are you doing, darling?" They embraced, wide smiles on their faces—Martha's eyes closed as she held the elder lady tight. "I'm doing fine, Grandma, I've waited a long time to see you again!" They reminisced about all the times they had talked at the market, and the time she phoned the inn asking to talk to Seth after meeting him for the first time. When she was ready to leave, she asked, "Grandma, will you ask Seth to come and see me? I'm afraid to call him, I know he's angry with me."

The next day Katie phoned her grandson. "Martha came to visit me yesterday, she's afraid to phone you, and she'd like to see you." He didn't say anything. Then she said firmly, "Go see her."

Reluctantly, he obeyed his grandmother, going to the market with a quivering stomach and a racing heart. It felt like his legs were going to give out when they stood face-to-face— he had no idea what to say to her. He wanted to embrace and kiss her, but the serious and troubled look on her face convinced him that wouldn't be welcomed.

He didn't know what to say, he didn't even know how to start the conversation. She said nothing, and just stood there. He noticed, out of the corner of his eye, her stern and intolerant father and brothers watching them from a distance. He finally asked, "How have you been?" She didn't answer the question, nervously turning to look at her father, then returning a cold stare to him. Her father called out, "Martha, come here, I need you to weigh these potatoes." As she started walking away, she quickly said under her breath, "Meet me at the lake at four o'clock."

He went there and nervously waited the two hours, dreading the thought of her not coming, but when the time came he was overwhelmed by the sight of her walking down the path. He noticed that she had changed—she was more mature, her movements more reserved and graceful, a kind of elegance, she was even more beautiful than before—her milky complexion, perfect features, full breasts and sensuous lips, and her dreamy blue eyes. At that moment he put it out of his head to pout and try to worry her—knowing he had pushed that issue too far, certainly as far as he could—stunned to his senses just in time—he knew he was very close to losing her, and he was scared he'd say the wrong thing. He felt he had to tell her, "You were all that mattered to me—you still are, but you left me, you went away. That hurt!" He desperately wanted to hear her tell him he was all that mattered to her. "Your schoolteacher came to visit and explained that she couldn't go into the whole story, but you had no choice but to go. It was hard not being trusted to know the whole story."

She said, "None of this was easy for me." He started to interrupt her, but she wouldn't allow it. "If you aren't willing to give me the time and space I need, then you don't love me."

He was hoping for a smile from her, but all he got was her eyes locked on his, he'd never seen her this serious. She said,

"I was told you were unfaithful to me while I was away." He froze, speechless while searching for a measured reaction—he wasn't going to admit his guilt if it meant losing her. She continued, "I know we never talked about it, and I know I had to leave without saying goodbye, but I just assumed we were gonna be faithful to each other." Racing through his mind was awful panic—he'd be willing to suffer any consequences for betraying her short of losing her, he had contemplated what his life would be without her, it scared him to think of the loneliness.

He pleaded, "I love you, and I wanna spend my life with you. I see more love in your eyes than any other man could ever see, and I know you'd easily find another one to love you, but you'll never find one who'll love you more than I do." He watched a gentle, subtle smile appear, and then an ever so slight nod. He walked toward her, hoping to embrace her, but she failed to react, and he stopped short. He thought she'd react warmer to his plea, but she could be unyielding—almost hardhearted.

"I was true to you, Seth. I want you to know that." She stood on her tiptoes and gave him a kiss, but only on his cheek. "If you want me, then you'll have to be faithful to me from this moment on." He pulled her close to him, holding her in his arms again after waiting so long. She said, "I think we both need some time, we have a lot of things we both need to do. I've been through a lot, and now that you're out of school you need to help your father with the problems at the inn." He slowly dropped his arms and stepped back, reassuring her, "I'm not gonna rush you, I'll give you all the time you need." She gave him a short kiss, this time on the lips. They held hands while they walked back to the market. All he thought about was how much he wanted to taste her—devour her.

She had a lot of time to think about him while away, and now was even more determined to prevent her church and family from trying to keep her away from him, and because he also had family problems, she worried that perhaps his family, not hers, would doom their relationship.

Once they knew their feelings for each other were still strong, they went to visit Katie, seeking guidance and reinforcement. She was overjoyed to see them, especially surprised that they came together. Martha said, "Grandma, this is the first time Seth and I have gone out in public together—we're getting brave!" Katie got serious. "Take your time, settle the issues with your families, if your love's strong enough, it'll stand all challenges."

Heeding Katie's advice, they decided, for now, Martha would stay living at home and work at the produce booth— Seth would continue to work at the inn.

Chapter 20

At the market Martha watched Jonas from a distance and with suspicion, aware he could be violent—she had experienced his outbursts. Seth told her long ago to stay away from Jonas, that he was capable of doing serious violence, but she wanted to find out more about him. She already knew he was a white supremacist, refusing to do business with African Americans, Hispanics, and Jews, and his market booth was a hangout for skinheads and bikers—tattooed, denim-and leather-dressed people wearing Nazi armbands and riding large and loud motorcycles. She figured he was selling guns to people who weren't supposed to have them, a lot of them were probably stolen, and because Bill Ganttrano was hanging around, drugs were likely being sold right there in the market. Jonas doing business with Ganttrano doubly scared Martha because the turmoil at the Oregon Inn gave Jonas opportunity to use him to harm Will and Seth.

She asked him, "Where's Hannah?" Jonas was surprised she came to his booth—he wasn't unhappy about it because he knew he had to start being nice to her if he wanted to spring his trap. He said, "She went to Florida to be with her mother. I think she killed Ben." Martha laughed at the ridiculous assertion. "She's too gentle a person to hurt anybody, even Ben. I'm glad to hear she got away from here."

Starting about the middle of September 1962, Freda, obeying Jonas's instructions, reached out to Martha to establish a friendship. Freda had beautiful, sparkling eyes, blue like Martha's—needed for membership in Jonas's club of horrors. Martha, using her detective prowess, decided to cooperate. She had suspected early that Freda was told to lure her to the Konrad farm. Martha wished she knew Jonas's timetable, she'd make sure hers supplanted his.

Freda questioned her. "I guess your church is pretty strict when it comes to doing it before you get married, isn't it?" Martha answered, "Yes, they're preaching that all the time in the youth group class." Freda asked, "Do you think people should wait?" Martha paused before answering, she wasn't sure how much she should tell about her and Seth. "We never went 'all the way', he knows I wanna wait until we're married, and my parents would be devastated if they found out we did it."

When Freda told Jonas that Martha was a virgin he was relieved. He told her he feared Seth and Martha having sex—that would contaminate her because he was half Italian. Hearing him say that convinced her that Jonas's racism and his twisted obsession with Martha were intensifying—he was drifting into insanity.

Freda fed Martha the information Jonas wanted her to know. "Jonas and me had been lovers until he found out I can't get pregnant, he wants children who will belong to the pure Aryan race that Hitler envisioned would rule the world."

Then she told the big lie, "Any woman he selects to have his kids—she has to be of German ancestry with blue eyes, and a virgin—all the things you are, will inherit the farm and all his money, which is a whole lot." She watched for Martha's reaction, watching for some kind of sign the girl would be interested in such an absurd and repulsive proposition. In reality, the plan was filled with violence and tragedy—Martha giving birth to children Freda would claim as hers. Freda was so desperate to have children—it no longer mattered to her how she got them, even if it meant that the young woman who actually bears them will be shot and burned in the oven when she's no longer needed.

Over the next month and a half, Freda confessed to Martha incrementally, tempting her with just enough information to keep her coming back. "He's got a small cult following at the farm, creepy guys he's found in homeless shelters someplace— Alfred, Sophia, and Rudolf supervise 'em." She waited for another day, and then filled her in some more. "They go find homeless people, bring 'em to the farm, Rudolf shoots 'em and Jonas and Alfred burn 'em in the oven. Then they throw their bones into a shallow pit they dug in back of the barn." Finally she told the horrible truth. "One of Jonas's ambitions is to somehow get Will Hartman to the Konrad farm, shoot him, and burn him in the oven." Martha was sure the same fate was planned for Seth.

While Freda was supplying all the deceptions, Jonas was keeping one from Freda—he'd give Martha the chance to cooperate. To him Martha was the plum, she also had the genes, and she was younger and much prettier than Freda. If she decided to willingly be his mistress, bear his children, and raise them with him, she'd be allowed to live. The bullet would go into Freda's head.

Chapter 21

Growing up at the inn had given Seth an overview how it was run before the advent of corruption. Now out of school and working there full-time, he was learning how it was being run now—keeping his mouth shut and his eyes and ears open—being unthreatening. As the next-generation Hartman, he'd have to learn every aspect of running an inn, develop a detailed plan, and then find help to wrest control of the place from the racketeers who stole it from his father.

Henrietta was the bridge between the organized crime and the Hartman family. She was the office manager, bookkeeper, and the boss of the kitchen and housekeeping staff. Sal also charged his wife with making sure the outlaws didn't get out of line or steal money. Sal trusted her completely, and rewarded her with the power to threaten or order harmed anyone she decided was her enemy.

There were times when Seth had bad feelings about her, he resented her loyalty to her mobster husband, the man making it possible for the criminals to wreak their havoc, including Bill Ganttrano and his lucrative drug-dealing operation. Seth was also unhappy with Henrietta arranging the love affair with Joanne.

However, he could never forget that he also loved her—she helped raise him, protected him, and taught him the many lessons of life. She was his mother's sister—reminded over the years by so many people how she was so much like Magdalena.

Showing the first signs that he could become a shrewd businessman, he instinctively began studying his enemies—the players in this drama of crime—Bill Ganttrano doing the enforcing, Eva supervising the prostitution, and Big John in charge of the gambling.

When Big John wasn't dealing cards, he was having sex with Mary Simmons—a short, fat, and foul-mouthed woman who worked at the inn as a barmaid. She lived in a trailer across Mexico Road from the inn with her husband Bill, choosing not to leave him because he got a monthly disability check from the Veterans Administration. Bill worked at the inn doing odd jobs and running errands for Henrietta and area farmers. He worked occasionally for Walter Dern, hired to dig up the house garden—the garden that Martha was supposed to tend.

Bill, almost always half drunk, started tolerating Mary's infidelity when he got emphysema and lost his ability to satisfy her in bed. She would humiliate him, bragging to the barroom patrons about her and John's interracial affair. "They don't call him Big John because of his shoe size!"

On Saturday afternoon, a couple of days after the Fourth of July, corrupt chief county detective Jack Gallo came to the inn to see one of the girls, he patronized the prostitutes and played cards at the inn regularly. Jack was a tall and slim good-looking man in his early forties. He wore his brown hair close-cropped on the sides, neatly parted and combed back into flowing waves, shiny from good smelling hair tonic. When Bill told him all the girls were in town shopping, he pushed his pointed finger into Ganttrano's chest. "I don't want to hear that shit, you better find me a blow job real fast." Ganttrano was desperate. He never had one of Sal's bullies rough him up, but he knew that'd probably happen if Gallo complained. "Go upstairs to Room 3 Jack—I'll send a girl right up." He hurried to his apartment where his current girlfriend was lying on the couch watching television. Stephanie was a cocaine addict from Baltimore, a young and cute street urchin with brown eyes accented with a heavy coating of black eye shadow and mascara. Her bleached blond hair was short, chop cut with erratic length, broken off from over bleaching. He turned off the television to get her attention. "I need you to go upstairs to Room 3 and give this pissed-off cop a blowjob." She jumped to her feet, and started screaming at him. "Fuck you, I'm no whore, you have a lot of balls asking me to do that!" He grabbed a handful of her hair with a firm grip, then slapped her across the face. She started crying. "I thought you loved me!" He slapped her again. "I do love you, and because you love me you're gonna do this for me. If this prick doesn't get what he wants, he'll close this place down and I'll probably get whacked." Stephanie went upstairs and turned the first trick she ever did—she did it for Bill. After Gallo left she came back to the apartment, lit a cigarette and fell back onto the couch. "How much did he tip you?" She looked up at him, then at the TV, ignoring the question. "Hey, I asked you a fuckin question." She reluctantly answered—"He gave me twenty dollars." He stared at her, waiting, and then ordered, "Give me the fuckin money." Pouting, she got it out of her back pocket, crumpled it and threw it at him.

Gallo was one of the more frequent players at Big John's card games, along with District Attorney Bryan Garrison—a huge, tall three hundred pound former college quarterback in his mid fifties, with black curly hair, and county judge Fred Bonner, almost seventy years old, short and skinny, a bald man with a beak nose. Other frequent players were wealthy attorney Henry Glass, Dr. Dick Sparr, an eccentric general practitioner with a serious gambling addiction, and Tommy Shane, a short, bowlegged washed-up jockey who trained Sal's race horses and fixed races for the mob. Shane weighed just over one hundred pounds, and looked older than his thirty-five years, likely from the rough living—he was frequently found sleeping in horse stables, usually evicted from some run-down apartment, or made homeless by a woman who had her fill of his mooching.

Unfortunately for Shane, he bet on horses running races he didn't have a fix on, making a habit of losing money he borrowed from Sal to get his alimony and child-support payments current enough to stay out of jail. Always being chased by loan sharks, and being arrested for petty theft numerous times, he'd burglarize filling stations and steal car batteries, and one time grabbed a crate of tomatoes from the Dern's market booth. Walter Dern ran after him until two young men joined the chase and snared him. Martha never forgot the look of desperation on his face as the police led him off.

The game that night began shortly after 10 PM, and in little time Tommy, a lousy poker player, was losing money, squirming and sweating as if his last dollar was on the table. During a break, Big John went upstairs and told Ganttrano, "What's the story with Shane? He's jittery, he's driving me nuts." Ganttrano explained that Shane was late making a loan payment. "Sal told him if he doesn't have the money tomorrow, he better figure out how to shit it."

Big John wasn't happy. "I told you before, I don't want desperate men playing in my games! It's dangerous, they can cause a lot of fuckin trouble!" Ganttrano told him not to worry. "I'll come downstairs and keep an eye on him and make sure there ain't any trouble."

About midnight, Shane, drinking heavily and losing big, charged John with trick dealing and accused the other players of signaling each other. "This fuckin game is rigged!" Everyone had enough of him by now—Ganttrano told him to get out. "I ain't leaving here until I got $5,000, that's what I gotta give Sal tomorrow. If I don't get it, I'm going to the cops and tell 'em everything about this sorry-ass place." Gallo spoke up, "I am the cops, and you ain't telling me shit!" Tommy shouted across the table, "You're a nobody, you're a fuckin half-assed cop, I'll talk to the feds, you prick!"

Ganttrano, reacting to Shane's latest threat, was trying his best to calm him. "Come on Tommy, let's go take a walk, get some fresh air, it'll help you relax, there's people here that'll help you if you just cool your ass."

As Ganttrano, Tommy, and Bill Simmons, walked down the path to the picnic grove, Ganttrano, walking behind the two others, pulled the axe used to chop wood for the dining room fireplace out of the chopping block and buried it into Shane's back. He fell to his knees, crying out, "No! Don't do this to me!" Simmons stood motionless, overcome with shock from seeing the attack, and now watching Ganttrano kick Shane in the head over and over. Moaning from the agonizing pain, he died in just a few minutes.

Just before most of the card players came outside after hearing the commotion, Ganttrano warned Simmons to keep his mouth shut or he'd get the same thing Shane got. When Judge Bonner saw the body, he turned to Ganttrano and shouted, "You're a stupid, crazy son of a bitch, somebody ought to commit you to a goddamn mental institution!" Then he told Gallo, "Get me the hell out of here." Bonner had sat on the bench for over twenty years, he'd taken bribes for years—mostly to pay his gambling debts—he'd played favorites in many of his rulings and had many powerful friends because of his political might. He also had enemies who would make sure he was removed from the bench and jailed when placed at the scene of a murder and an illegal card game.

The next morning an angry Sal showed up to see Ganttrano. "I got told yesterday the justice department is investigating illegal gun dealing over at the market, so now they're gonna be snooping around and poking their noses in the shit I'm doing here." He was clearly agitated. "So what the fuck do you do, you kill one of the stoolies they're looking for! For all I know, he was an informant, it's gonna piss 'em off bad if they find out he's dead." Ganttrano, trying hard not to panic, didn't know what to say, so he said nothing. Sal kept ranting, "They're federal, so the locals can't help us with these pricks, they wanna talk to Tommy about race fixing and money laundering, sooner or later they're gonna come here looking for him, so you better tell 'em he skipped town, and you better make sure his body never turns up." He warned, "If they discover his body and find out he owed me money, they're gonna come after my ass. I'm gonna to be their chief murder suspect, and if they do you're a dead man, I promise you that." It wouldn't take much more going wrong for Sal to explode into a violent rage, maybe even pulling a gun and shooting somebody, maybe Bill Ganttrano. "The only thing that's saving you—I'm pretty sure Tommy was gonna rat me and everyone else out, so its good he's fuckin dead." He noticed Ganttrano's look of relief. "Don't think you're out of the woods you prick, you're an idiot, you're just a lucky fuckin idiot."

Bill knew he had to stay calm, think things out, get rid of Shane's body and do a thorough cover-up of the murder. His own survival depended on it.

The next day at market Martha noticed Ganttrano chain-smoking and nervously pacing about while talking to Jonas. She was able to overhear some of the conversation—Jonas ordered one of his soldiers to take his truck to the Oregon Inn later that night and meet up with Ganttrano.

At sundown she began yet another dangerous adventure into the night—she got into the back of Jonas's truck and hid under the tarp. After the bumpy ride to the inn, Ganttrano and the guard pulled back the tarp, lucky for her not enough to expose her, just far enough to throw Shane's body into the truck. She was scared, daring not to tremble, staying completely still and taking shallow breaths for maybe ten minutes—it seemed like an hour. She heard Ganttrano's clanging, loosely hinged lighter torch another cigarette, and after a long drag and exhale, she listened to his bragging. "Losers who loan money to gamble sooner or later have unhappy endings, I had to put an axe in this asshole's back."

When they threw the corpse into the truck it landed right up against her. They had wrapped Shane's bleeding head with a towel, now almost completely saturated with blood, and a blanket around his upper torso to catch the blood that was oozing from the wound in his back. Using only her thumb and index finger, Martha partially unwrapped the blood-soaked towel. Aided by moonlight just bright enough, she saw it was Tommy Shane's dead face with a congealed look of shock and horror. She waited until the truck slowed and turned down the lane at the Konrad farm, then slipped out from under the tarp and lightly slid off the tailgate, landing on her feet, she had to start running to gain her balance, hurrying across the darkened meadow to get to the springhouse to witness Ganttrano and the soldier unload the body while the chained dogs gave their loud vicious greeting.

A few days later Marberg, still working on the gun-dealing investigation, came to the market and questioned some of the workers about the murder of Ben Kaiser, and now the disappearance of Tommy Shane.

He introduced himself to Martha, and then asked her to walk outside with him. "I got a phone call from the Orbachville police, they told me the parents of one of your schoolmates up there, a boy named Jason, was having nightmares about some man attacking you. He broke down and told his parents that he rescued you." Martha noticed Marberg's obvious self-confidence, his coolness while digging for information, she realized for the first time how much easier it is to investigate a crime when citizens are willing to help the detective. Marberg continued, "I know the man who attacked you was Ben Kaiser, and that gives you a motive for murder." Martha felt faint—she quickly walked over to a bench and sat down. He continued, "Miss Dern, may I call you Martha?" She nodded, still trying to calm herself. "I know you didn't kill Mr. Kaiser, what I want to know is why he came up north to see you."

She gave an answer much more expansive than he was expecting. "I have information that'll shock you, information that I was eventually gonna take to the police."

Marberg suggested they meet the next day at her house—he wanted to tape record their conversation. She agreed to the meeting, she knew she'd need to bargain with him right away because when he found out Tommy Shane was murdered at the inn she figured he'd raid it, and after discovering everything else that was going on there, close it and sell it at a government auction. "I'm not gonna give you any information, or testify in court, unless I get a deal trading mobsters, politicians, and Nazis for the Oregon Inn free and clear—no seizure of the inn and no criminal charges against the Hartmans." He smiled, impressed by the young, strong-minded girl, then gave the answer she had wished for and prayed to get but never imagined would come so easily. He said, "OK, if you got what you say you got, we'll deal."

Trusting him to do what he promised, she described the first time she had looked in the farmhouse window, and seeing two dead bodies. She described Ben Kaiser attacking her, and how she hid her injuries from everyone but Jason and her close friend Elizabeth. She told him Tommy Shane was dead, and told the details of riding in the back of Jonas's pickup truck while Ganttrano and the soldier hauled Shane's body to the Konrad farm, and that she heard Bill Ganttrano confess killing him.

She said, "I'm serious about what I want in return for my testimony. I'll lie and deny I know anything if you go back on your word. You can even send me to jail, I'm gonna do whatever it takes to protect my boyfriend and his family." Marberg was convinced she meant what she said.

He said, "Look, I know all about what's been going on at the Oregon Inn—gambling, prostitution, there's probably also a lot of drugs, that's easy. What I need is your eyewitness testimony to help me prosecute Konrad for harboring arsonists that burn down synagogues, and buying and stockpiling guns he knows are stolen. Those are federal crimes—I can put him away for a lot of years. He explained, "My best chance is to prosecute these guys for civil rights violations and antiracketeering laws. If we find evidence of murder—so much the better." She didn't like the sound of that. Murder was the worst of any crime and she felt that should be Marberg's priority.

She said, "Tommy Shane's body was taken to the Konrad farm all right, but nobody's gonna find it buried there."

Marberg looked puzzled. "What did they do with it?" She said, "I told you I had information that will shock you—Jonas Konrad and his fellow Nazis burn people in this giant oven he has in the back section of his house! That's what they were doing with those two bodies I told you I saw! I'm sure that's what they did with Shane's corpse. After they burn the flesh they throw the bones in a pit in the back of the barn, many of 'em have been carried off by wild animals." Marberg's jaw dropped. "That's hard to believe. What could possibly be his motive for doing that?" She knew his motive. "Hate. He's preparing for the Nazi's return to take over the world. He's expecting to be appointed boss of America!" Marberg couldn't help laughing at such a preposterous scenario, but noticing she wasn't laughing, his face quickly turned serious. "He's got to be insane." She nodded. "You're telling me he's baking people after killing them, this stuff you're describing is really bizarre. If I go in there with a warrant searching for an oven and nothing's there, I lose everything—I get him for nothing, not for hate law violations, not for gun trafficking, not a damn thing, he'll close down everything and skip town and I lose all the evidence." She said, "I get it now, you don't trust me—you think I'm making this all up!" He answered, "It's not that I think you're making things up, it's just that I need to be sure you saw what you think you saw because the only search warrant I'm going to get is one handed down by a federal grand jury, a body that has more power than any judge. However, because it has so much power, it demands convincing and flawless testimony, or I don't get my warrant. If I do get the warrant, it'll only be good for the things I tell them I'm looking for. If I discover anything else, with very few exceptions, I'm out of luck." He noticed how attentive she was to his every word, feeling sure she understood how critically important details are to an investigation—he knew she was a smart girl. "I'd have to be crazy to go to a county judge—no judge in this county is going to give me a warrant without Judge Bonner finding out, and then he'll order a cover up real fast to protect himself and his cronies being implicated in Shane's murder."

Martha respected Paul Marberg's sense of logic and perseverance. She decided to cooperate with him—to a point. Marberg's fortunes were getting even better. Bill Simmons, now sober for the longest period in years, phoned him to make a deal—he was anxious to testify against Ganttrano and provide the names of the card players who were there the night Shane was murdered. That loaded Marberg's cannons, he went to see Judge Bonner and DA Garrison and offered them a deal. Cooperate or be placed at the murder scene when Tommy Shane was killed. He needed their cooperation so he could live up to the deal he made with Martha. They both readily agreed—they wouldn't be indicted for conspiracy as long as they guaranteed the Hartmans and their inn weren't bothered.

Bonner phoned Sal. "Get everybody and everything out of there, this detective Marberg has me and Garrison by the balls." Sal told him to calm down. "Don't let this dick head rattle you." Bonner was screaming now. "He can have me removed from the bench, or worse—they'll crucify me!" The judge was frantic. "He's going to twist your balls too if you don't shut down and get everything and everybody out of there." Now Sal believed Bonner. He phoned Eva and told her to get the girls out of the inn and out of town, then called Big John and told him to go home to New York and never come back.

At the Konrad farm, Jonas, the insane psychopath, stripped Shane's body, placed it in the oven, and incinerated it, throwing his bones into the pit.

Ganttrano, suitcases packed, went to the Konrad farm to collect the last bit of money Jonas owed him. He had made enormous profits from drug dealing and had enough money for a long vacation. He couldn't resist boasting despite Jonas's disinterest. "I was the man who made Sal and his associates hundreds of thousands of dollars, and I'm the guy who supported the Hartman family, preventing 'em from losing the inn."

Jonas, tired of listening to him, pulled a pistol from his pocket and shot him twice in the head, then stripped him, removed his jewelry, and burned him in the oven. Jonas couldn't allow Ganttrano to leave town knowing what he knew. Ganttrano burned for hours.

Chapter 22

Seth knew nothing of Martha's deal with Marberg to prevent the seizure of the Oregon Inn, and he didn't know Bill Ganttrano was dead. He walked from one room to the next, the barroom, the dining room, and then upstairs down the hallway. Bill was gone, Eva, the girls, and Big John were gone, he asked Henrietta if she heard from Sal, Seth knew something was up.

Henrietta said, "I've been trying to get in touch with Sal all day, I think either something very bad or something very good has happened." Seth was scared, and he noticed the look of despair on his aunt's face. She said, "I think I'll go upstairs and wake your father. Somebody could be on there way here to harm him. I'll bring him downstairs where we can keep an eye on him. Seth, the time for you to take over has arrived."

He felt prepared to take charge, as ready as he would ever be.

The next day he went to the Country View Nursing Home and told Katie to pack—she was going home. She had been fully recovered for some time, but had opted to stay and reside in the assisted living area, a refuge from the inn's chaos. Her grandson now changed all that. "I need you there—the inn needs you now more than ever."

A few days after getting Katie settled in and back to work, Henrietta came to him to discuss her future. He had mixed feelings about her, loving her as a son does, disturbed with her because she had been so loyal to her despicable husband, disappointed because of her un-acceptance of Martha, and finally angry at her for being naïve and using poor judgment getting Joanne involved in his life.

Then it was the normal sexual attraction most adolescent boys have while growing up, dreaming about making love to older women, even an aunt—he dreamed about her plenty. He wondered how odd it actually was for nephews to recognize how slim and good looking an aunt is. She wore clothing and shoes that were the latest fashion, her black hair slightly teased into the latest style. For a fleeting moment he wondered how it'd be to act on those youthful fantasies now that he was in control. She was pleading to him to let her stay, she had to get away from Sal, Seth knew he could become as loathsome as Sal and Bill Ganttrano, he could prey on her. He could punish her for being alive while her sister—his mother, was dead. Seth Hartman could easily become a monster.

He witnessed at an early age relationships that enriched a person's life and those that destroyed. He'd be content only taking from Aunt Henrietta more of the good she had given him over the years, now hoping to give some of it back to her and Katie. He hoped his good behavior wasn't just acquired, but also genetically based—increasing the odds that he wouldn't later succumb to immorality.

Seth said, "As long as you're married to Uncle Sal, I can't allow you to stay here. I'm sorry, but that's the way it's gotta be." The next day she phoned Sal and told him she was going to file for divorce. He hung up on her. She was relieved. It was Sal's way of divorcing her—immediate.

Chapter 23

Marberg came to the Dern farm for the interview with Martha. She brought from her bedroom twenty-seven pages of handwritten notes detailing everything she knew about Jonas Konrad, Ben Kaiser, Freda Koller, and others, and how she saw Jonas and Ben place a body into the oven when she peeked in the farmhouse window. She described how Kaiser came to Orbachville to scare her into keeping her mouth shut. She wrote about Tommy Shane's murder, how his body was placed in the back of the pickup truck next to her, and she told of Freda detailing Jonas's plan for a pure Aryan race in America.

After giving Marberg the pages of notes she said, "This is all I know, everything I can testify about. If something should happen to me, you have it all." She felt a good feeling of accomplishment.

She asked, "Would you need a warrant to raid the Konrad farmhouse if you were told someone was being held captive there?" He only knew her for a short time, but he was already familiar with how her mind worked. He said, "I'm way ahead of you, sweetheart, don't even think about doing something stupid." He was being firm and serious. "I won't allow you to do anything that'll risk your life—I could lose my job."

She had her mind made up. Waiting for Jonas to find the courage to kidnap her could take a long time, so she reasoned if she forced his hand she could have him brought to justice a lot quicker. Also, she didn't want him to get off on a technicality because something was discovered during a raid that wasn't listed in the warrant. If it were reported to the police that a crime was taking place, that she had been kidnapped and was being held prisoner, they could raid the farm without a warrant. Anything discovered during the raid could be used to prosecute Jonas and the other fanatics because the police would now have probable cause to search the entire farm.

She said, "I can't see how you could lose your job, you're not responsible for what I do, and there aren't any witnesses sitting here." Marberg was starting to get angry. "I'm not going to allow you to risk your life—this Jonas Konrad is evidently a madman, I'll lock you up first!" She yelled, "I'm already in danger, I've been in danger for a while! I've been attacked, and I'm gonna be attacked again—killed." She kept shouting for emphasis. "Do you think an eighteen-year-old girl should be used to make babies and then be killed?" Marberg comprehended the horror of it all, and could understand her being scared—he spoke up forcefully, "Of course not—but I can't allow you to risk your life doing my job!" He gave a loud and firm response because he knew he was up against a very stubborn young woman.

She got quiet, then said softly. "I'd appreciate you coming quickly if someone phones and tells you I'm being held against my will." Pretending not to hear her, he walked out the door.

That night she couldn't sleep, dozing off a few restless minutes at a time, and when morning finally came, Rebecca, noticing Martha's disheveled appearance, asked, "Are you in trouble again?" She was hoping for a reassuring answer but it didn't come. "Mother, I need you to do me a favor." Rebecca cautiously agreed.

"Seth is driving his dad to the doctor, he'll be gone all day, and I need you to give him a very important message when he gets back and comes to the market to see me." To Rebecca, it was already beginning to sound scary. "Where are you gonna be?" Martha lied. "I'm going to church to help the teachers get ready for bible school." Rebecca was happy and surprised to hear that her daughter was helping at church.

Martha had picked this day, Seth being away assured her he wouldn't get in the way until she wanted him to. She gave her mother the message. "Tell him to check the coffee can, that's all you got to tell him, he'll know what to do." Rebecca, believing any message that seemed like a code involved danger, asked, "What's he gonna do?" Martha was becoming impatient, she was scared, but restless to get started—she gave her mother a quick kiss on the cheek and ran out the door without answering.

She walked along Mexico Road to the inn, finding Katie sitting in the kitchen peeling potatoes. "Martha, my darling Martha! I'm so glad to see you!" She reached out as Martha bent over, and they hugged and kissed. "Grandma, I need you to phone someone if you don't hear from me by midnight—it's very important. She went out into the dining room and wrote down Marberg's phone number on a paper napkin. "Here's his phone number—ask for Paul Marberg. Tell him to come and get me—he'll know where I am. If he's not there tell whoever answers that its urgent Marberg gets the message." Katie stood up, reached out and held her tightly as if she wasn't going to let go. "Does Seth know what you're doing?" She didn't answer that question. "Grandma, I'm also leaving a note for Seth telling him to call Marberg, but the thing is he won't do it—he'll come for me himself and there won't be any stopping him. I gotta tell him where I am because he loves me, but I need to rely on you to call this Marberg guy, he's a detective." Katie responded with shock. "Detective! Martha, I know you have to do what you have to do, but maybe you should wait and take Seth with you—whatever you're planning to do, don't do it alone!" Martha got up to leave. She said, "I got to do it alone, nobody else can do it."

She started crying after she left the inn, lifting up her long dress and using it to wipe away the tears while hurriedly walking to the hideaway. She removed the sod and lid from atop the coffee can, and placed a note to Seth inside. Exhausted from lack of sleep, she dozed off sitting under the tree where they had shared so much time together, awakening without a sweater to a chilly nighttime air. The sounds of chirping crickets, croaking frogs, and hooting owls, muffled by the cold thick air, stayed with her as she shivered while walking to the Konrad farm pretending to use darkness for cover, in reality now wanting to be seen.

Alfred, with the help of two of the soldiers, quickly captured her—grabbing her and knocking her to the ground, using duct tape to hold her ankles together and tie her hands behind her back. He pulled a handful of her hair so hard some of it was torn from her scalp, then twisted and jerked her head and neck as the soldiers wrapped more tape around her head and over her mouth, pasting down her ears and hair, allowing just enough opening at her nose to breathe. While waiting for further orders they threw her around the room. They were a lot more violent than she had expected.

Then they were ordered to take her to a room that had crudely cut sheets of plywood nailed over the windows, the only light coming from a single light bulb dangling over a wooden table and two old wooden chairs. Sitting in a corner was a white porcelain chamber pot with lid—it had a strong smell of the pine oil mixed with water and the urine.

Jonas and Freda came into the room and looked down at Martha helplessly lying on the floor crying. He was stunned when Alfred told him she was at the farm. "Welcome to my chamber, I never expected you to walk to my house—I thought I'd have to force you here!" He used a long knife to cut away the duct tape over her mouth. "You came here uninvited to spy on me just like you did before, now I know for sure that you're my enemy—oh but such a beautiful enemy!

Freda was clearly bothered by his pining over the young girl. He left the room and Freda tore away most of the tape still sticking to her, then helped her into one of the chairs. "You better do what he says, or he'll hurt you bad." She added, "He's gonna ask you what you told the police."

Martha, needing to get the most information as fast as she could, asked "I thought his plan was to get me pregnant?" Freda, not knowing if Jonas was listening from the hallway, whispered, "He doesn't think like normal people. He's gonna rape you, for him it has to be rape. He has to hate you. If you're agreeable he can't exploit you, he only gets satisfaction if he's exploiting somebody. The best thing for you to do is keep your mouth shut and give in to him, he won't kill you if things are going according to his plan—getting you pregnant." She asked another hurried question. "What happens when I get pregnant?" Freda said, "He'll get you pregnant again, then a third time, maybe a fourth time."

She repeated what she had told her before when talking at the market, the big lie, the lie of all lies, the lie that was the ultimate betrayal. "If eventually you want to be his wife you'll live here raising his and your children—becoming part of our community." Stunned when told Jonas actually believed there was a chance she'd cooperate—she stopped crying, now rage was quickly churning up into defiance. "He'll have to kill me because I'll never give in to him—even if I did they'd come to get me anyhow, they'd never give up until they found me." Freda said, "When they come, and if you tell 'em you're a prisoner, or if you run away, he'll kill the children—his and your children—and burn 'em in the oven—even if they're still babies!" Martha screamed, "You're a liar! I'm not stupid, he's gonna kill me and you're gonna raise the babies. I'd never live here with him and all you crazy, sick people. If I was willing to do that he'd kill you, not me—I'm the one he's in love with!"

Freda clenched her fist and punched her in the face once, and then again. "He's gonna break a lot of your bones, then he's gonna kill Will Hartman and your boyfriend. He has a lot of scores to settle." She started punching her again—she kept at it a few more times, and then continued her rant. "He's gonna control you until it's time to destroy you—in a month, a year, five years from now! And you thought Hannah was your friend. Ha! She was going to be your midwife! She was in on the whole thing!" Martha recalled Hannah left after her husband, Ben Kaiser, was murdered—maybe she wasn't as committed to the cause as Jonas believed. Freda said, "Now it'll be Sophia, cruel, vicious Sophia! It won't be so easy with her."

Freda's punches were causing Martha to bleed from her mouth and nose—her left eye was beginning to swell up. When Jonas came back into the room he told Freda to leave and close the door. "How terrible to bruise such a beautiful face. I think Freda is jealous of you." He slapped her, and then closed his fist and took his turn punching her face. She was spitting blood, crying loudly, and then screamed, "If you want me so bad why are you hitting me?" A twisted, contorted expression of grief moved across his face. He began to weep, and then fell to his knees and begged, "Please make love to me, let me father your children, we'll have perfect children, they'll be the ultimate tributes to your beauty. I love you!"

Reminding himself yet again of the impossibility of her ever wanting him, he jumped to his feet. He put his hands around her neck, and with extraordinary strength lifted her up off the chair and tossed her onto the table, then used his knife to cut away her dress and rip away her bra and underpants. Being naked revealed serious bruises from Alfred and the soldiers roughing her up. Being undressed in front of him made her feel dead. Feeling fear and panic, she realized she couldn't escape and was no longer in control. Injured and exhausted, she was unable to resist even though she desperately wanted to.

He started punching her again, now blood was gushing from her nose. She shook her head to ward off unconsciousness.

He spoke softly, almost in a whisper. "I have waited so long to get inside you, I'm gonna have you every day, you're too beautiful to spend life on a farm smelling of chicken shit, milking cows, feeding hogs and working your ass off in some potato patch. And a barroom is no better, that half-breed boyfriend of yours will pimp you to keep that fuckin hotel afloat."

He undid his belt and walked to the edge of the table as his pants and underwear fell to his ankles, his shirt covering his genitals—he looked hideous. He put his hands under her thighs, bent her knees and pushed her legs back to lift her up, then drew himself up against her.

Martha held her breath, wincing and waiting to feel him enter her, but she felt nothing. He was just standing there, staring at her. Finally she cried out, "What are you waiting for?" He didn't answer.

"You can't do it, can you? After all the violence, after all the twisted dreams in your deranged mind, you rub yourself up against me and you're not man enough to fulfill your fantasy—getting inside me!" He tried to ignore her taunts while still trying to get aroused. Finally he gave up. She spit in his face and he punched her in the face again, then another time. Now her eye was completely swollen shut, the other one starting, her face bruised and covered with dried blood and tearstains, her nose and mouth were seeping blood through the clots. She growled, "You can't do it with any woman you're in love with because you only get satisfied when giving pain instead of pleasure." Then, no longer able to resist, she screamed, "You're a sick, pathetic man, possessed by hatred. Doing it with you would be like doing it with Satan!"

Jonas finally was convinced Martha would never want him. For that she had to be punished—he'd kill her. He called out for Freda—she opened the door as if she was standing just on the other side. "Get my pistol and have 'em fire up the oven." She hesitated and looked puzzled, wondering why he was going to kill the girl now. "Do what you're told! I've changed my mind—I'm not going to breed with this pig-dog!"

Martha was huddled on the hard table, her knees pulled up to her chin, arms wrapped around her legs in a vain attempt to hide her nakedness.

While the horrifying thoughts were swirling around in her mind, she suddenly recalled Seth telling her about his father encountering Nazis taking suicide pills. She wasted no time. She asked, "Where do you keep your pill?" Jonas, looking surprised and puzzled by her question, asked, "What pill?" She desperately hoped he had studied Nazi suicides, and decided to mimic them. She answered, "The suicide pill Nazi 'big wigs' take when the end is near—and the end is near for you. They'll be coming for me, they have no choice but to come for me, and when they do, they're gonna discover your oven and the bones of your victims!"

A look of anguish flashed across his face. "You dirty bitch, you're only worried about laying with that half-breed—you're a goddamn whore! When he gets here I'm gonna put the barrel of this pistol in his mouth and blow his brains out. Then I'm gonna kill his old man, that son of a bitch, and finally you're gonna burn in the oven after I shove this broomstick up into you." She was convinced that no man could be sicker than he was, unable to sexually abuse her using nature's way, he was ready to use a broomstick to assault her in a cruel and vicious way.

Knowing she was running out of time fast, she screamed, "Take the pill, Jonas! Take the pill!"

Seth returned home with Will and then went to the market. Rebecca gave him the message. "You're to check the coffee can." She began crying frantically. "I think she's in danger, I don't know what she's doing, but I'm really scared."

He had never seen Rebecca like this, especially her accepting him as a link to Martha—she was a typical Brethren woman, serious and conservative, who usually kept her emotions suppressed. He tried his best not to panic, but terrible thoughts started running through his mind. He ran out of the market and got into his truck, speeding off the parking lot, and aiming it toward Mexico Road. He got to the path leading to the hideaway, jumped out, leaving the motor running and headlights shining. Running down to the big tree, he pulled the coffee can out of the ground, retrieved her note and ran back up to the truck to read it by the dim dome light in the cab. "Seth, please call detective Marberg at 555-3287, tell him to come to Jonas Konrad's farm, I'm probably being held captive. Please always remember that I love you—Martha."

He raced to the inn and yelled to his father to get in the truck—"We need to go get Martha." Will asked, "Where's she at?" When he told him she was at the Konrad farm, he jumped out of his chair, grabbed his shotgun and was stuffing shells in his pockets as he raced out the door. The sight of Will mobilizing only stirred more fear in Seth—his father responding like a soldier—it was instinct, imbedded deep in his makeup by West Point and combat. Seth had never witnessed it, only heard about it. In just an instant and during a crisis, he found the respect for his father he had sought for so long.

When they got to the farm two other soldiers approached them before they could get out of the truck. Will, pointing the shotgun at them, said, "If I were either of you, I'd get as far away from here as fast as I could. Things are going to be happening that you don't want to be involved in." They had assumed that somebody sooner or later would be coming to rescue Martha—they didn't want to be there when the shooting began, or when the police showed up. They accepted Will's convincing advice and began with a hurried walk, then started running out the lane to Mexico Road.

Will kicked in the door to the house and came face to face with a frightened Freda standing in the hall pointing to the room where Martha was. With Seth right behind him, he kicked that door in, and they found a surprised and shocked Jonas standing in the middle of the room holding two pills in one hand and his pistol in the other, his pants still around his ankles—a pathetic sight. Martha screamed, "Seth, stay away from him, he'll kill you!" He was horror-struck when he saw her bruised body and bloody, battered face, but somehow he kept his rage in check. While keeping his eyes on Jonas, he slowly took off his shirt and threw it to her so she could cover herself.

Will spoke slowly, "Give me the pistol Jonas, it's over." Jonas began weeping—still holding tightly to the pistol in his right hand—the pills in the clenched fist of his other. Will slowly handed the shotgun to Seth, then told Jonas, "If you hate me as much as you say, if you feel you must kill me, then do it, but if you do, my son is going to empty both barrels of that shotgun into you. If that's what it's going to take for him and this here girl of his to be safe, then I guess you and I'll have to pay the ultimate price."

Jonas dropped the pistol and raised his hand with the two pills to his mouth. Will, who had lived through this before, took a stretched leap toward him, slapping his hand away, the pills flying across the room as they both fell to the floor. Will landed on top, then knocked Jonas out with one punch, then used most of the remaining duct tape to wrap him up like a mummy. Seth ran to Martha, she was shaking and crying hysterically.

A few minutes later Paul Marberg and about a dozen deputies raced in the farm lane, breaking down the farmhouse's front door. A news reporter, who got a tip, followed the raiding party—the newspaper covered the story, using large headlines and the entire front page to describe the discovered atrocities. Marberg told the reporter he had received a phone tip from a woman named Katie Hartman telling him a young girl named Martha Dern was being held prisoner at the Konrad farm.

That bit of information was for the newspaper, but there was more to the Paul Marberg and Martha Dern story.

When he walked into the room Martha was still shaking, Seth had her wrapped in a blanket he kept in his truck—they were waiting for the ambulance. She saw no sign of emotion on his face, typical for him, a desired trait for a tough criminal investigator—no feelings for victims or witnesses that could cause messy friendships to develop, nothing like that.

This girl was different though. He knew that. She could determine to help or hurt somebody, she could be a rowdy tomboy and she could be dainty feminine. She wanted to be this guy's girlfriend, standing there with her, he loves her but probably will never be able to completely figure her out, even while she loves him back and has his children. Because she can be so focused on what she wants, she doesn't care what anybody, including Paul Marberg, thinks of her, whether he likes or dislikes her—whether he is or was angry with her or not, that's not important. All that's important is that he keeps his word. He had met his match. He allowed himself to become emotional, taken aback when he saw her swollen-shut eye, the black and blue marks, her bloody punched up face.

She said, "Don't give me a hard time, I've had enough problems for one day. My dress and underwear is laying on the floor in shreds, I'm naked under this blanket, and I'm bleeding and hurting just about everywhere." He wouldn't have admonished her even if he wanted to—Seth was standing there trying to find somebody to punch in the face.

A couple of the deputies took Jonas away handcuffed. Freda had gone out the back door, running with Alfred, Sophia, and Rudolf into the woods as fast as they could. They were all captured. All the low level underlings had scattered when Marberg and his entourage sped in the lane—everyone was gone.

Martha spent three weeks in the hospital in Rossville being treated for two broken ribs, a broken arm, and severe lacerations and bruises on her face and body. Seth and Rebecca stayed by her bedside—Will and Katie spent hours there—even her father came to visit. Her brothers came with their wives.

A criminal forensic team launched their investigation, working for weeks trying to determine how many bodies were actually shot, burned in the oven, their bones thrown in the pit in back of the barn. Shane and Ganttrano's remains were the first found and identified.

The government confiscated thousands of pieces of Nazi and KKK literature. Jonas's tax records were audited and his gun sales records were examined. Jonas, along with Freda, Alfred, Sophia, and Rudolf were tried for murder, tax evasion, drug trafficking, violating gun laws and civil rights laws, and some other lesser charges, they were sentenced to life in prison without any chance of parole. The Konrad farm was seized and auctioned by the government.

Sal was arrested for racketeering—illegal gambling, promoting prostitution, and tax violations. He was sentenced to fifteen years in state prison.

Martha's eyewitness testimony, along with Bill Simmons', made the convictions possible.

When Martha came home from the hospital to continue her convalescing, Rebecca allowed Seth to come to the house when Walter and the boys were in the fields or at the market. He was always prepared to dive out her bedroom window if any of them came home unexpectedly, or if any church people came to visit unannounced.

Seth and Martha spent the days reading—he mostly read books about American history, she was still addicted to the murder mysteries that still had to be hidden under her mattress.

Chapter 24

Katie decided to give the inn a thorough cleaning—it hadn't been done for years. She had kept the inn spotless when she ran it—the guest rooms, the dining room, the kitchen, everything had always looked and smelled fresh and clean.

At 6:30 AM on a Monday morning Katie had the inn's sound system blaring her favorite hymns. They could be heard a mile into the woods and down Mexico Road:

> *God of our Fathers, whose almighty hand,*
> *Leads forth in beauty all the starry band,*
> *Of shining worlds in splendor through the skies,*
> *Our grateful songs before Thy throne arise.*

She opened every window, allowing a strong chilly fall breeze to blow far into the rooms, She said, "Soap can wash away the dirt and grime, but the hymns will clean the air—blow the stench of evil right out the windows!"

Her helpers, three young girls and an elderly gentleman, hired to help clean, cook, and wait on tables, diluted three five-gallon pails of pine oil concentrate into buckets of scalding hot water and mopped and wiped the floors, walls, and furniture. Windows were cleaned—yellow cigarette smoke stained curtains were washed, and tablecloths and towels were laundered, the worn out ones replaced.

Will had taken over tending bar, shooting pool with the customers, talking sports—club soda now his beverage of choice. Henrietta was now renting out the rooms and working as dining-room hostess and office manager. Family dining, especially Sunday dinner, featuring German and Italian dishes, was once again featured. Seth was helping everyone—learning everything about the business.

Martha's life was returning to normal. She had started to help her mother with the household chores. She was far behind other Brethren girls her age learning to be a wife and mother. Those girls by now could cook, sew, mend, and handily tend babies.

In late October, after the harvest—the green cornstalks becoming yellow sticks, and the orange and brown leaves starting their drop to the ground—it was time to do the canning of fruits and vegetables. Martha never understood why it was called canning—the foods were put in glass jars, then boiled and vacuum-sealed. "Shouldn't it be called 'jarring'?" Rebecca replied, "Why do you ask such questions, who cares what it's called—jarring, canning, jarring, canning!" Their laughter underscored their joy spending time together—more than ever before.

One crisp morning, before sunrise, the kitchen was filled with farmwomen boiling jars and cooking the different foods to be preserved—it was hard work, going on until late that night. Martha did her part while learning a lot from the older women.

The next morning while Rebecca was sitting at the table having a cup of coffee, she looked up and saw tears flowing down Martha's cheeks, the tears she always knew would tell her that Martha was leaving home. Martha asked, "Will you help me pack a bag or two?" Rebecca had accepted long ago that her daughter would leave not only her parent's home like a grown child normally does, but also leave the church and her family's way of life. She knew Walter was going to be very disappointed—he'd take it as losing his child—but she believed her daughter had a right to be happy. "I'll help you, just take what you need for a few days until you get settled in. You can come back for more later."

They reminisced while packing some clothes, photographs, her Bible, birth certificate, and other personal tokens, then they sat at the table and ate breakfast. "I'll drive you over there, but I'm not gonna tell your father I did." Martha said, "Mother, you don't have to, don't make problems for yourself." Rebecca responded firmly, "I want to drive you there." Martha reached over to hold hands with both of hers. Looking at them through the tears, she held them up to her lips and gave them a gentle kiss. "Mother, I love you so much." They stood up and embraced. "I think it's time for me to go now."

When Martha got out of the car in front of the inn, Katie— she was sweeping the porch, walked over and greeted them, and then noticed the suitcases sitting on the ground. "Are you moving in?" Martha nodded. "If Seth will have me." Katie opened up her arms to give the nervous young girl a gentle hug. "My grandson isn't crazy, of course he'll want you here with him and his family. He's wanted that for a long time."

Katie found Seth in the kitchen replacing a leaky seal on the dishwasher. "There's someone outside to see you, she has her suitcases with her." He looked up and dropped the wrench, slipping and falling on the wet floor as he raced outside. He stopped short and saw the worried look on her face. "I hope you don't send me away because I'm hopelessly in love with you and I don't have any place else to go." He took her hand and ran to his truck, dragging her along. She asked, "Where are we going?" He didn't answer—pulling out so fast he threw white stones from Mexico Road across the inn's parking lot, blowing the truck's horn nonstop as he raced down the road. She slid across the truck seat and snuggled up against him.

Laughing loudly when they got back, she asked, "Why did we do that?" Seth, running and jumping in the air, shouted, "Because now we can be seen together, I can kiss you, hold your hand, hug you, and I can do crazy things with you like speeding down Mexico Road."

Katie was standing on the porch watching her grandson's excitement play out. Martha said to her, "I'd like to help out at the inn if I could, I want to learn to cook and I can clean, but I'm not gonna make any babies with him until he marries me." Katie laughed. "We'll discuss the wedding plans with his father after you get unpacked, and you can start work tomorrow."

Henrietta came out on the porch and greeted her with a hug—she had come to accept Martha was going to be part of the family. As the three women started for inside, Seth yelled, "Hey, where am I supposed to put her bags?" Nobody answered. Henrietta looked at Katie, then at a still nervous and unsure Martha. Will, standing in the doorway, yelled, "Put them in your room, she didn't come here to rent a room, she came here to live with you!" He picked up the bag and ran past the women and Will, up the stairs to his room.

A few evenings later Lester and Kay, hearing Martha left home to live with Seth, came to the inn to have dinner and visit. They were getting married in three months—Seth was going to be Lester's best man. After dinner, the two guys took a walk while the girls chatted. Martha, anxious to make friends with women her own age, listened open-eared as Kay told her about her life and her and Lester's plans. "I go to classes at night plus work full time as an accountant—my family still can't believe I work for this successful accounting firm." She lit a cigarette and took a long drag. "I didn't know about you when Seth was hanging around Lester's cabin." Martha didn't want misplaced guilt to kill a friendship before it started. "Seth and I have agreed not to talk about the stuff he did while I was away." She took another drag, her exhaling was much like a sigh of relief—her nervous smile turned to a warm relaxed one.

Lester always liked playing the role of a braggart—he had outgrown being a real one. "Take some advice from a stud, don't pamper her, she's a very sexy chick, but don't let her know it, just dick her brains out every chance you get." Seth let him go on—Lester was having fun. Seth couldn't resist asking, "Is that what you do to Kay, 'dick' her brains out?" Lester was quick with his answer, "Hell no, she's got too many brains—she screws my brains out!" Their laughter echoed through the woods while they shoved and pulled at each other.

Lester had never seen Seth so happy. "I know you're in love with her, you've been for a long time. I never understood that until I fell in love with Kay." Seth was glad Lester and Kay got together, she had matured him and he had mellowed her wildness and gave her self-confidence. Lester asked, "Are you coming in her? Kay and I aren't using condoms anymore, hell, we're getting married and want the first kid popping out as soon as possible!" Seth responded, "Kids don't just pop out you idiot, and it's none of your business whether I'm coming in my girl." Lester said, "I know you are, the girls that go to her church use that rhythm method, certain days you can and certain days you can't, and it's not fool proof. As soon as you get married get her on the pill or you're gonna have little kids in shitty diapers running all over the inn." Now, almost back to the inn, Lester gave some serious advice. "Tell her everyday that you love her and don't make your life with her so goddamn complicated." They shook hands and then wrestled each other to the ground, rolling around, pinning each other down and exchanging headlocks, just like they always did.

Martha helped Kay's sisters with the wedding, and Kay taught Martha how to shop for clothing—she had stopped wearing her bonnet and began wearing shorter dresses and skirts. They went to Rossville to buy jewelry—a thin necklace, a watch—skirts, slacks, blouses, sweaters, pantyhose and casual and dress shoes. She had never worn high-heeled shoes—she liked being taller. She started wearing a small amount of makeup and dark wine-colored lipstick that highlighted her beautiful sensuous lips.

She also bought records—country music, rock 'n' roll, big band music, and gospel songs. Seth bought her an expensive floor-model record player for their room.

Martha felt fortunate to have Kay as a friend, someone she could confide in during this period of her life changing. They were sharing the most intimate details about their relationships. She learned Kay had burned both ends of the candle while growing up—it was truly amazing that she became such a wonderful woman. Her grandparents, her father's parents, were a positive influence on Kay. The only child of an only child, she confided to Martha, "I'll eventually inherit their farm, when that day comes it'll double the size of the next-door Noll farm."

Martha told her how rebellious she was while growing up. "My family wanted me to marry a man who'd help on the farm, but I was always a daydreamer, I wanted to be a detective, a nurse, a teacher, or maybe even a doctor, then I met and fell in love with Seth and decided to share his dream."

Seth and Martha were making love most nights, sometimes all night. He would kiss her everywhere—she was a quick learner, returning his kisses and wrapping her arms and legs tightly around him, lifting her body to meet his, and when she felt him inside her she helped set the pace.

On February 9, 1963, a sunny but bitter cold day, Seth and Martha were married. The elegant, formal wedding's music included Mendelssohn's *Wedding March,* Bach's *Jesu, Joy of Man's Desiring,* and Katie's favorite hymn, by Martin Luther—she considered it the best ever written:

> A mighty fortress is our God, a bulwark never
>   failing—
> Our helper He amid the flood of mortal ills prevailing.
> For still our ancient foe doth seek to work us woe—
>   His craft and power are great—
> And, armed with cruel hate, on earth is not His
>   equal.

The ceremony was marked by the absence, with three exceptions, of the bride's family and friends. Rebecca chose loyalty to her husband over standing for her daughter—a terrible choice to be forced upon a mother. The bishop had excommunicated Martha—her father disowned her—her brothers and their wives, her cousins, her friends from church and school, they all condemned her for leaving the church and marrying Seth. Practically all Seth's distant relatives also stayed away—they weren't pleased with the newspaper headlines and accounts about the Oregon Inn. It would take time to restore its good name. Martha's attendants—the older women Katie and Henrietta—and Kay, her maid of honor, wore fine gowns of tangerine taffeta with high necklines and puffy sleeves, matching picture hats, white pumps, and carried bouquets of white carnations.

Martha wore a traditional white-veiled wedding gown with a long train and high-heeled open toe shoes with thin straps. Her hair was pinned up and pulled back from her face—she wore soft subtle makeup and long dangling pear-shaped earrings. She was a beautiful bride.

Just before it was time for her to walk down the aisle, Katie opened an old wooden jewelry box and gently removed an antique pearl necklace. "This necklace belonged to Sarah Hartman—I'd like you to be married wearing it, as I did." Martha was speechless, but then did find the words, "Katie, I'd be honored to wear the pearls."

The men wore black tuxedos. Will attended Seth, the church sexton stood in as the needed third groom's attendant. Lester served as best man.

As she was walking down the aisle Martha noticed sitting in attendance Emily, the teacher whom she had always trusted. Jason came along—he had helped save her. Then, taken aback, she saw Aunt Julia sitting there!

The ceremony was held in the same Lutheran Church where Reuben Hartman served first as land donor, then congregational founder, and finally as organist and choir director. Legend has Reuben Hartman wanting it named St. Paul's Lutheran Church because of the apostle Paul's commitment and sacrifice, who, after accepting Jesus as his Savior, spent the rest of his life delivering the Christian message to those who had never heard it.

Here, with a tall spire on its roof, an eight-foot wooden cross hanging behind the altar, and an organ that vibrated the pews, Seth's ancestors worshiped and were baptized, married, and mourned. The minister offered prayers and proclamations, asking God to bless the holy matrimony of this young couple.

The Hartman family, known for its large weddings attended by hundreds of family members and friends, was now celebrating one with only twenty or so guests. It was tragic that the bride, so innocent, and with unmatched beauty, had to give up her family to marry her prince.

After the ceremony the small gathering celebrated at the inn with a grand dinner, then with good conversation and later dancing—all in traditional Pennsylvania German style, but also with Mediterranean influence—the inclusion of Italian pasta and sweets prepared by Aunt Henrietta.

Katie stayed near Emily, Jason, and Aunt Julia, ensuring they felt welcomed. Aunt Julia asked if there was a room at the inn she could rent. Not wanted by her son and his wife, she needed a place to live and a job.

Chapter 25

On February 3, 1968, at Seth and Martha Hartman's fifth-wedding-anniversary dinner, attended by over one hundred family members and friends in the inn's dining room, Will Hartman gave the toast.

"To my son Seth and his wife Martha, to their son Will II, standing right here in front of the podium in his suit, bathed and smelling good, his hair slicked down and combed thanks to his mother—he's four years old, so you won't see him looking like this very often, to their daughter, two-year-old Maggie, sitting over there next to her mother in her frilly dress and black shiny sandals, and to baby Katie, sleeping in her father's arms, born this past December—may the blessings from God continue for this much-in-love couple and their children."

Will looked at Seth with pride and added, "My three grandchildren have been sent to us from heaven, although my daughter-in-law must be given credit for the labor of it all!" That remark produced laughter from the audience. "Years from now, after they've served as patriarch and matriarch of this great family, and the next generation or two decides to pass judgment on them, they'll surely rule that Seth and Martha Hartman lived their lives with an unshakable love and commitment to each other." And that remark brought applause from the audience.

Will Hartman had lived in the throes of deep, dark, depression. He wept when he lost his wife, struggled through combat and the failures as an army officer, and then gave in to drugs and alcohol. He regretted his failure to accept his responsibilities as the next Hartman in line, but he had been back for a long time now, he had become the bridge for his son to cross and take charge.

It's natural to want the spirit of your offspring to be an extension of your own—your heart aches at the thought they might suffer, but to allow their success to flourish, even amid setbacks, is the stance that sanctifies life.

www.ingramcontent.com/pod-product-compliance
Lightning Source LLC
Chambersburg PA
CBHW032144020726
47496CB00003B/702